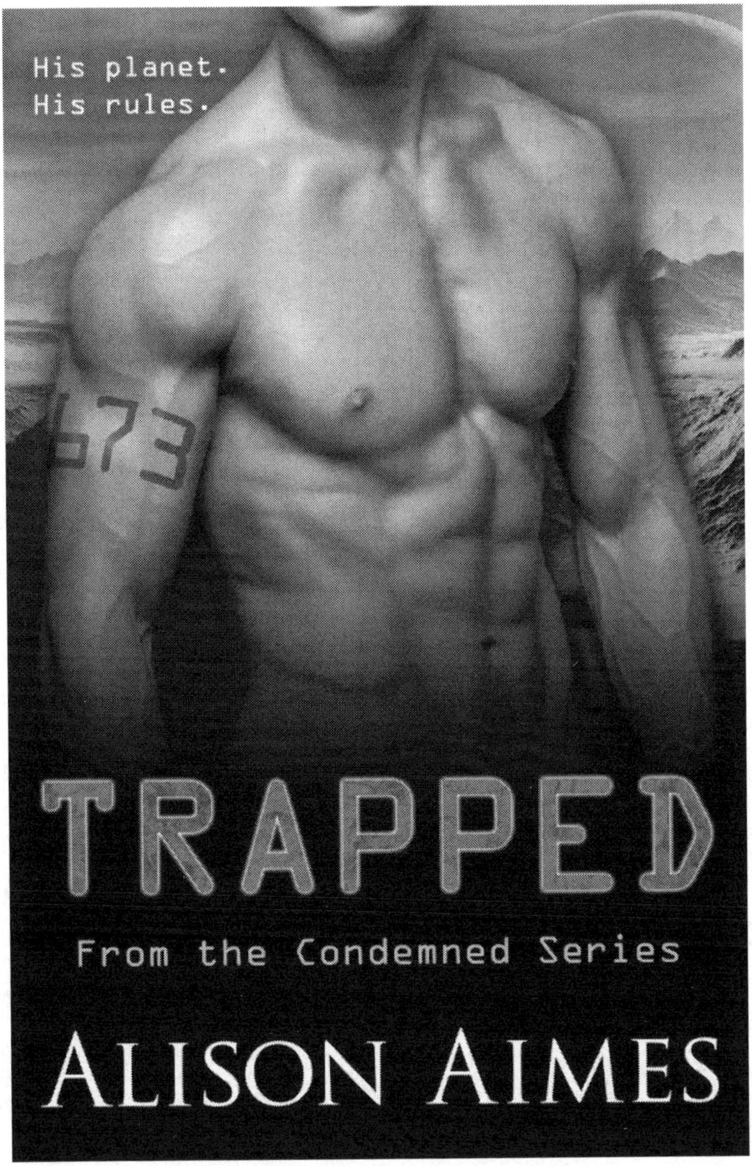
His planet.
His rules.
673
TRAPPED
From the Condemned Series
ALISON AIMES

Copyright

Trapped
Book One in the Condemned Series
Bookmark: Copyright
Published by Orchid Publishing
Copyright 2015. Orchid, Inc.
Cover by Patricia Schmitt
EPub Edition ISBN: 978-0-9964683-0-5
Print Edition ISBN: 978-0-9964683-1-2

Excerpt from TAKEN copyright © 2015 by Alison Aimes

This is a work of fiction. Names, characters, places, and incidents are products of the author's imagination and are not to be construed as real. Any resemblance to actual events, locales, organizations, or persons, living or dead, is entirely coincidental.

This work of fiction is licensed for your personal enjoyment only. It may not be re-sold or given away to other people. If you would like to share this book with another person, please purchase an additional copy for each person. If you're reading this book and did not purchase it, or it was not purchased for your use only, then please return it and purchase your own copy. Thank you for respecting the hard work of this author. To obtain permission to excerpt portions of the text, please contact the author at www.alisonaimes.com

Interior format by The Killion Group
http://thekilliongroupinc.com

TRAPPED
Book One in the Condemned Series

Alison Aimes

TRAPPED:
Book One in the Condemned Series

Cadet Bella West has one simple objective when she joins the scientific mission to Dragath25, the notorious penal planet housing Earth's condemned. She will accept any risk to enable her siblings to share in the disappearing resources reserved for Earth's elite. But when her shuttle crashes, her simple mission becomes complicated fast. Now, to stay alive she'll have to depend on one of Dragath25's own. But such protection doesn't come free.

Convicted of a crime he didn't commit, ex-soldier Caine Anders has become more beast than man after eight grueling years on an unforgiving planet of dirt and rock—and even more treacherous inhabitants. He doesn't look out for anyone but himself and he certainly never grows attached. So when the bold female offers him pleasure in return for protection, he takes the deal without hesitation. He never expects how her touch will alter him. Or the growing realization that saving her may be the key to his own salvation.

But caring for someone on Dragath25 may be the greatest hazard of all.

Warning: This full-length HEA novel is a sizzling romance with a hot alpha male and a strong, determined woman, but it begins with a transactional deal for sex in return for protection. In the beginning, the hero holds more of the power and control. Reading how that changes—how a prisoner who's become more animal than man rediscovers his humanity—is part of the fun. But the sex is explicit, the story intense, and the uneven power dynamics at the start will not be for everyone.

ACKNOWLEDGMENTS

Special thanks to Patricia Schmitt for her gorgeous cover. Kim Killion for mad, beautiful website skills. Jennifer Jakes for her superb formatting abilities. And last, but not least, Danica Sorber for her exceptional, tireless, and brilliant PR work. Without her, I'd still be trying to figure out Facebook and using smoke signals to spread the word of the book's release.

Equally profound thanks to Briana St. James, Naomi Hughes, Jacy Mackin, and Arianne Cruz for their amazing editing help. You are all brilliant and insightful and I appreciate all the ways you made this story stronger.

Thank you, too, my beautiful, supportive kids whose tolerance and humor about my writing process makes me smile, my wonderful dad whose unshakable support aids me in ways you can't even imagine, and all my extraordinary friends and family who never looked anything but convinced when I said month after month that the book "was coming soon."

I'm pretty sure there are not enough thank yous in the world for my mom Barbara. Your incredible support is only surpassed by your superb and thoughtful editing. You've been there with me through every step and there's as much of you in this story as there is me. Thank you for every long phone call, every murmur of support when I was doubtful, every unbelievably quick turnaround, and every brilliant idea and suggestion. You rock.

Finally, thank you Kurosh, my real life hero. Thank you for your support. Thank you for your help. Thank you for your strength and your courage and for showing me what being in love is all about. Thank you for being the kind of man who inspires and encourages and for taking my dream seriously and demanding I believe in it, too. You can't know how much that gift means to me. Love you always and forever.

Happy reading, everyone!

CHAPTER ONE

9015

The shrill blare of a warning alarm snapped Cadet Annabella West to attention. With a hasty shove, she secured the last of the test tubes in the storage bay.

"Nothing to be concerned about." The pilot's calm voice crackled through her military-issued helmet.

She gave it a smack to smooth out the sound. Like so much of her other mission gear, the darn thing had been rebuilt so many times it was barely functional.

She refused to consider what that meant for the worn shuttle parts themselves. What was the point? Technological know-how might be better than ever, but resources had been practically non-existent even before she was born. She awarded the helmet another not-so-gentle tap.

"Just some stronger than expected atmospheric change." The rest of the pilot's statement came through loud and clear. "Best to find a seat for the duration of the flight. Entry into a planet's atmosphere is always a bumpy ride."

"You can sit next to me, Cadet West." Junior Officer Pogue, lead military soldier for the Winthrop-Humanity research mission, patted the space next to him on the narrow steel bench used for landings. A leer played on his face. "I'll strap you in good and tight. I love a good-looking woman crisscrossed in leather and metal."

A rumble of laughter sounded from the line of brawny soldiers settling beside Pogue.

Assholes.

Bella moved past with her spine ramrod straight, her heart beating faster than she would have liked.

She'd always had tremendous respect for the soldiers who kept her and the rest of the scientists safe, but Pogue and his crew were proving harder to like than most. Still what could you do? Four thousand light years from Earth, the Council's strict rules, and fifteen weeks from the space station she and the others currently called home, there wasn't much recourse. Especially without risking Command Council's attention.

"Don't let them get to you." Senior Council Officer Dr. Jim Winthrop was head of the scientific team of the expedition and the highest ranking officer aboard. He offered a reassuring smile as she settled beside him, his head jostling up and down as the ship swayed. The movement made the intricate Council designation of linking Cs behind his right ear look like little more than a blurred smudge. Ironic, really, given its import. "You excited?"

"Excited. Terrified." She rechecked the closures on her grey uniform before tightening her straps—and noticed her hands were shaking. *Damn.* She laced them together on her lap and pasted on a cool smile. Until now, she'd been able to keep her dislike of closed, tight spaces out of her file. "I hope we find something useful."

"While I hope we don't run into any inmates." Cadet Davies' mumbled comment came from across the aisle, the flare of warning lights painting her helmet and the visible portions of her face in shades of green and yellow. Still, the colors couldn't camouflage the worry staining her dark eyes. The same worry Bella was trying her best to hide.

Like Bella, Ava Davies was a junior research trainee who'd only recently graduated from the Council Academy Science Department. But that was pretty much where the similarities between them began and ended. By the end of their first year, Cadet Davies would be well on her way to earning a high level Command Council Officer ranking, a position Bella could never hold.

Her future superior seemed competent enough, but they'd had little interaction. During training, Davies had lived with her kind in Council housing rather than the crowded barracks, only bothering to show up for classes when she felt like it.

Must be nice. But then again, Davies hadn't come to the Academy on a scholarship. If she got kicked out, she had a wealthy, connected family to fall back on. If Bella screwed up, she and her siblings would starve.

"The penal colony is three hundred metrals from the planet center," soothed Dr. Winthrop, his voice vibrating along with the ship. For a Council descendant, he was friendlier than most. "Our landing site is six hundred metrals in the opposite direction. We'll touch down, obtain available vegetation and soil samples, and be back in flight before the planet's inmates are the wiser." Breaking protocol, he reached over and squeezed Bella's gloved hand, his dark-green eyes crinkling. "Standard mission practice. Don't worry."

Bella's gaze found Davies'. Her colleague raised one eyebrow. Bella needed no translation. Davies had noticed Winthrop's interest was more than mentor-mentee. Luckily, she appeared more amused than condemning. Still, as subtly as possible, Bella shifted her hand closer to her thigh.

Jim Winthrop might be a smart, good-looking guy with more decency than most of his kind, but he was still Council, her superior, and frankly she wasn't looking for any kind of personal complication. She'd scrapped and sacrificed to make it past the Academy's rigorous screening process to train to become a junior level scientist, the highest position a non-Council descendant could achieve outside of marriage to a Council elite. She couldn't afford any mistakes, especially the one night-and-done kind that might jeopardize her position. The Council wasn't known for its forgiving ways.

"You two will see." Dr. Winthrop leaned forward in his seat. "You're about to be a part of something historic. Mark my words."

"That would be amazing." Davies smiled, but it didn't reach her eyes.

Bella understood. It was hard to imagine this mission was going to be the one to succeed after so many expeditions with better leads had failed, but who knew? With billions of Council and non-Council inhabitants already lost and more dying every day, any lead, however slight, was worth investigating.

"We've entered Dragath25 air space. Ensure your straps are fastened tight." The pilot's voice again sounded through her earpiece. "We'll touch down in ten."

"I hate this part." Their communications specialist Steve Meyers shot her a weak smile from his seat to her left. Like the majority of lower level skill personnel, all the soldiers, and Bella, there was no Council designation behind his ear. "But closer to the front of the shuttle is definitely the better spot. Less turbulence."

Bella gave him a commiserating grimace and sucked down a few slow, deep breaths as the shuttle shuddered. She saw a couple of the other scientists looking like she felt. Terrence, who'd placed himself next to Davies—per usual—was green. Poor guy. He'd thrown up almost every space drop, and this was rougher than usual.

She glanced into the rear of the shuttle and bit back a frown. The soldiers were pains in the ass, true, but they'd get the roughest part of the ride back there. Hopefully, none of them would get space-sick. On landings like this, soldiers were vital. While every research mission had an element of danger, landing on a planet at the outskirts of human territory known to be chocked-full of violent criminals seemed particularly insane.

And yet, if Dr. Winthrop's hypothesis was correct—and this was a big *if* since travel to Dragath25 on droid transport was always a one-way ticket for prisoners only—there might be a portion of the planet that thrived despite the brutal weather conditions. No one knew for sure since early records related to the planet's settlement had been destroyed during the Great Wars and ensuing chaos. But a few droids had recently returned with intriguing vegetation samples stuck to a tread or a stabilizer. Subsequent droid reconnaissance had yielded promising possibilities, though nothing absolute.

Which was why she and the rest of Winthrop's team were here.

If such findings proved real, Dragath25 might actually offer humans hope for survival. Hard as it was to imagine, what had been established over two thousand years ago as a human dumping ground for the worst of the worst might end up offering a new crop of hardy plants that could save a dying Earth. Energize the dwindling numbers who'd been forced to live in crowded, dusty ad hoc settlements near the last remaining rain collection reservoirs. And, if Winthrop's optimistic musings were to be believed, restore humanity—now firmly under Command Council rule—to something akin to what it had once been when plants and water were in abundance.

So why did she have such a bad feeling in the pit of her stomach?

A set of ear-piercing bells shrieked through the cabin. The warning lights imbedded in the hull flared to red. "Emergency landing protocol initiated." The pilot's voice was no longer so calm. "We've encountered an unexpected electrical disturbance. At first, it appeared to be a simple atmospheric change, but now—"

His words cut off. Ominous static crackled along the line.

Bella's gaze locked with Davies'.

The ship dropped.

Bella came awake with a gasp.

Dizzy. Disoriented. Pain beat at her chest and shoulder as she forced her eyes open. Blaring alarms only added to her confusion.

One look around and everything crystallized. The crackle of fire. The blur of smoke. The sweet scent of blood and the acrid scent of burning flesh. *Oh no, oh no, oh no.* The shuttle had crashed. Fracture lines snaked through her helmet obscuring visibility.

Frantic, she yanked off her helmet and squinted through the smoke. Fumbling with her straps, her siblings' gaunt, hopeful faces slammed through her mind. They were depending on her.

A scream strangled in her throat. To her left, Steve Meyers' sightless eyes stared back at her through his visor, a trickle of dried blood tracking from his nose.

She scrambled free of her restraints, tripped over a mangled piece of steel two inches from her boots, and lurched across the aisle, her hands landing on warm thighs.

A palm closed around her wrist.

"Cadet Davies?" she screamed over the shrill alarms. "Davies? Can you hear me?"

"West?" The word was a moan, but it sent Bella's heart soaring.

"The ship crashed. We need to get out." She was already feeling her way along her colleague's straps for the release. "Are you hurt?"

"I–I don't know....My head hurts. My leg, too."

"We'll take a look once we're out." Bella's hand slipped from the restraint. To Davies' right, Terrence stared back without blinking, his neck twisted at an impossible angle. The poor man. He'd never moon over Davies again.

"They were right. I–I shouldn't have come." The woman's voice was oddly monotone, her arms hanging limply by her sides as if she didn't care if Bella found the release or not. "I–I was wishing for death, and now look what I've done."

Bella's head snapped up. "This isn't your fault. There was an accident."

Knocked off-kilter, Bella forced herself to concentrate on finding her colleague's release latch. Under normal circumstances, she'd have pushed the woman to explain. Davies was a part of the privileged Council elite, after all. Death should have been the furthest thing from the woman's mind.

But now wasn't the time to probe.

The rough nylon sliced the pads of Bella's fingertips as she worked to find that damn release.

Finally, a click. Davies was free.

"I'm going to put my arm around you," Bella instructed. "Lean on me—and try and stay low."

She gave a small silent thank you when the woman's arm circled her waist and they were able to stagger together into something between a squat and a stand. Bella's shoulder screamed as Davies' weight pressed against her, but she pushed the pain aside.

"Bella?" A hand shot from the smoke to grab her arm.

She jerked to a halt. "Dr. Winthrop?" She didn't use his first name despite the fact that he'd used hers. Command Council protocol was very clear on that point.

"I'm…I'm hurt." Winthrop's voice shook. Not a good sign.

"We'll help." She tried to keep the alarm from her voice. "We need to get outside. Fast."

"You should go." Shock left Winthrop's voice oddly matter of fact. He jerked off his helmet with trembling hands. "The fire's getting worse."

"You're coming, too." She swiveled toward Davies. Her colleague had removed her helmet to reveal a nasty bump on her forehead and one of her legs was definitely not working right, but her eyes looked infinitely clearer than they had a second ago. "Davies, can you make it to the back exit without me?"

"Let me help." The woman's sincerity was easy to hear. As was her pain.

"Get to the exit," insisted Bella. "That's the help I need. We'll be right behind."

The woman grabbed her shoulder, her voice low. "Let me try. It shouldn't be you who dies in here."

"No one else is dying." Bella gave the woman a soft push, surprised and touched that someone like her would even make such an offer. "Go." When Davies still refused to move, Bella grew less gentle. "You're only slowing us down. Go!"

She'd deal with whatever repercussions came from addressing a Council member in such a fashion later…if they all survived.

Davies' lips flat-lined, but she didn't argue. Or grow all haughty. Mouthing one more *don't die* warning, she simply hobbled away, her awkward hopping gait instantly swallowed by the thickening smoke.

Bella swiveled back to Winthrop. "Can you get up?" Her fingers flew over Winthrop's restraint straps, tugging, wrestling, searching for that damn opener. It gave way with a beautiful click.

Her arms came around Winthrop's waist, her left side instantly wet. Blood. Enough to soak her clothes. She forced a smile and heaved. "You need to help me."

His head lolled, his chin cracking into her temple. He was nearly dead weight in her arms. They'd never make it.

"Dr. Winthrop? Please?" Her voice splintered. There'd been too much death already. "You need to focus. You need to stand up. Now."

No response.

"Help." Faint at first, the plea from a few paces ahead grew louder and louder with each panicked bark.

Propping Winthrop back into his seat, she scrambled forward, waving away the thick smoke, deliberately avoiding looking at the two dead soldiers on either side.

"My belt's jammed." The minute he saw her, Officer Pogue threw himself forward, trying to tear out of the restraints. "I can't get out." He kicked his boot toward something on the ground in front of him. "There's my knife. Cut me out."

Seizing the knife with two hands, she hacked at the restraint. "Stop struggling. I'll get you out."

"Faster," he urged.

Then with a final slice, the fraying restraint gave way. Pogue popped up on a roar. "Let's go. The fire's burning fast."

"Wait. You have to help me with Dr. Winthrop. He can't walk on his own."

"No time. He'll never make it anyway." Pogue turned away.

"No." She sprung at him, sinking her nails into his shoulder. She'd put up with his constant harassment because non-Council descendants stuck together and because he was a decorated soldier with useful survival training. She needed that expertise now. They all did. "I didn't leave you. Take Winthrop's arm. Put him between us. We can make it."

When he still didn't move, she grew desperate. "Do it. Or I'll tell the Council you refused to help one of their own. Think your life will be worth anything after that?"

Pogue's jaw tightened and, for a terrible second, she thought he might strike her, but then he was striding past her, knocking her thigh into the bench, plowing his shoulder into Winthrop's stomach, and hoisting him upward into a fireman's carry.

"Go," he shouted.

Knowing he was right behind, she scrambled forward.

A moan came from the right.

She swiveled toward the sound, but Pogue's big body rammed into her, making her stumble. "No more. You'll get us killed. Keep moving."

"But—"

"Go. Or I'll leave you and your precious Council admirer." Pogue barreled into her, shoving her hard.

"We can't just leave the others here to die!"

Without another word, he slammed into her again, sending Winthrop's boots into her hip and her sprawling forward on a pained gasp.

"Move or I'll run right over you."

That cowardly bastard. He'd begged her to save him, but refused to do the same for anyone else.

"Bella? Is that you? Bella, you're almost there." Davies' terrified coaxing echoed from up ahead. "Come on."

Hating herself, hating Pogue, Bella stumbled down the aisle. The burn in her throat had become agony, breathing difficult. Pogue was hard on her heels, ready to stampede over her in an instant. On either side, dark smudges taunted her with the possibility of other sightless eyes.

"You made it." Soft hands grabbed hold of her arm, guiding her through a twisted hole in the wreckage she hadn't even seen.

Bella's knees hit the ground. Her head snapped up and she sucked in dry, hot air. Two orange suns blazed high in the sky. All around her, desolate rock and dust swirled in a tapestry of bleak browns and rust as far as the eye could see. Even the sky was the color of dried blood. No hoped for vegetation in sight.

The trip had been for naught.

Pogue jogged by her, an unconscious Winthrop still in his hold. "Move away from the shuttle," he roared. "It's going to blow."

Several soldiers followed. Apparently, Steve Meyers had been wrong. This time the back of the shuttle had been the place to be. At least ten of the military team still lived while everyone from the scientific team besides her, Davies, and Dr. Winthrop had perished.

Her gaze locked with Davies'. They shuffled away from the burning shuttle. "All those deaths for nothing."

A loan tear tracked down her colleague's soot-covered face. "But we survived."

An inhuman shriek rent the air.

Everyone froze. Eyes wide, the soldiers' guns shot up, pointing wildly at the rocky outcroppings where anything could be hiding.

The hair at Bella's nape prickled.

Yes, they'd survived. But for how long?

CHAPTER TWO

"You can't just leave them here." A woman's furious voice reached prisoner 673 through the rocky canyon. He froze. Cocked his head. Inhaled, but scented nothing except the usual arid scent of dirt and dust.

After so many years alone, the sound of such loud squawking was jarring. And that the voice was a woman's? His cock twitched and rose, taking notice. Eight years was a long time to go without. The last time the droids had dropped a woman on Dragath25 was five years ago. 225's pack had gotten hold of her first. She'd lasted five minutes.

It was a good reminder. Fragile things didn't last here. And nothing, not even long overdue pussy, was worth risking his survival.

"You hear those shrieks? They're coming." An equally enraged male's voice boomed through the canyon, thoughtfully telegraphing his precise location. "Our shuttle streaked through the sky like a clear come-and-get-me invitation for the entire penal population of murderers and psychopaths. We don't have time to dick around. We don't have time for those who'll only slow us down. We're moving out."

"You coward. I saved your life. The least you can do is try and return the favor."

673 cleared the canyon in time to see a bull of red-haired soldier dressed in fatigues grab a far smaller woman in a

torn grey uniform, her boots dragging along the ground as he shook her hard.

673's whole body went tight. He didn't like bullies. He dropped into a crouch. Instinct taking over as he slunk forward, his gaze absorbing everything. The way the soldier bastard favored his right side. The large firearm strapped to his holster. The second weapon at the man's back. The way the woman's ripped uniform clung to her curvy body and the outraged rigidity of her spine even up against a man twice her size. The nine other thick-necked, smug soldiers with similar military-issued buzz cuts standing close by, no clue of the danger he represented, their sole attention on the woman.

In the next instant, the woman dropped into the dirt. On a perfect, heart-shaped ass.

Freezing in place, 673 waited to see what happened next.

"Fine," the woman shouted, stumbling to her feet. "Go. But I'm not leaving. We'll find a way."

"Your funeral." Soldier bastard grabbed a pack off the ground. He slung it onto his shoulder next to a similar one.

"At least leave us one." She surged forward, grabbing for the pack, but soldier bastard darted out of reach.

"Not so high and mighty now, are you, Cadet West? In fact, seems like you and your Council-friends might need us after all." Soldier bastard patted the pack. "These were issued to the military crew, and you know how strict Command Council is about ensuring resources are relegated to the proper department. You survive the night, I'll be ready to hear just what you're willing to do to get an unsanctioned taste." With a final leer in her direction, soldier bastard kicked it into a jog. "Let's go, men."

An odd frisson of uncertainty snaked through 673. He wanted those weapons. Wanted what was in those packs. But he'd come for a different reason entirely, and with the seven soldiers out of the way, the few left would be easy pickings.

It was a curious thing: choice. For so long, there had been only the option to survive. He didn't like having alternatives. It almost made him feel human again.

"West, please," a dark-haired female in a similar grey uniform limped over to where the other woman stood, the quality of her boots marking her as Council even without his ability to see the CC designation on her skin, "go with them. You've done so much for us already. Why should you die, too?"

He'd already noted this second female and the wounded Council officer on the ground and dismissed them as any kind of threat. Fact was, like fighter girl, they were dead folks walking—because, in this case, soldier bastard was right. The strong barely survived out here. The injured didn't have a chance in hell.

His fighter girl didn't seem to care, though. *His?* No, she wasn't his. She wasn't anything but Dragath25 dirt in the making.

He'd learned long ago not to stick his neck out for anyone else. Keeping himself alive was hard enough.

Just beyond, the wind picked up, brushing against 673's skin, signaling the start of another dust storm. Within the half hour, this place would be choked in dirt and debris, everything within suffocated under an indifferent cloak of dirt and rock.

"I'm not leaving you." Fighter girl stumbled forward, her wavy, soot-colored hair brushing her ass…so easy to grab and wrap around his wrist. "Let's find something I can drag Dr. Winthrop in."

She turned in his direction, giving him his first full view of wide green eyes, a lush pink mouth, and firm, high tits full enough to fit his hands.

His body rioted to attention, the man he'd once been waking with a silent roar as white-hot lust flooded his veins. He jerked to standing, all subterfuge, all caution, forgotten. The absence of touch for eight long years a sudden agonizing stab of need across his skin.

"Look!" She pointed near to where he stood, and for a heart-stopping moment, he was sure he'd been sighted. But then she turned back to her friend. "There's something that looks like a cave only a little ways up. If we can make it there, we can hide."

"But—"

"No but. We are making it there." She dropped to her knees beside the wounded officer's body. "No one else is dying. Headquarters will send search and rescue to investigate the crash. We only have to stay alive until then."

The shrieking cry of 225's pack sounded again. Closing in fast.

The reminder cooled 673's lust enough to get him thinking again.

His gaze flickered between the woman, now frantically working with her friend to wrap the man in some kind of fabric, and the strewn, burning wreckage that littered the ground. His hands clenched and unclenched.

Choices.

His dick was telling him one thing. His mind another. *Shit.* He really hated choices.

He started forward.

"Wedge the cloth under his side." Bella dug her fingers beneath Winthrop's back and fumbled for the other side of the shirt. They'd found it flapping on a piece of wreckage. She didn't even want to think about where it had come from. "I've almost got it."

Another one of those horrifying shrieks shook the air. Louder than before. Her heart slammed into her throat. The wind seemed to be picking up as well. Larger and larger pieces of rock and dirt pinged against her skin. This place was even more inhospitable than Earth during its frequent dust storms.

"Just a little more," she urged. "I—"

"Oh, shit." Davies' panicked curse had Bella's head jerking up.

She promptly fell on her ass. Her mouth opening in a silent scream as terror strangled in her throat. The rock was alive and swaggering toward them, a rust-colored mammoth monstrosity that swirled dust and danger in its wake.

She blinked again, and the rock became a man. A massive, sculpted, dark-haired man. One wearing little more than a loincloth and boots, every inch of his muscled skin and face caked in mud the same reddish color as the rocks. Threat emanated from every pore.

The planet's inmates had found them.

She scrambled backwards on her ass, Davies right beside her. The man was at least a head taller and several inches thicker than Pogue, the biggest and strongest of the soldiers on their mission. The urge to jump and run pumped through every sinew, but Davies couldn't. Her colleague's leg wouldn't hold her more than a few steps.

Eyes locked on the approaching threat, Bella's fingers scraped the dirt behind, scrounging frantically for some kind of weapon. A rock. A piece of wreckage. Anything that might slow him down as his shadow fell over her and his wide shoulders blotted out the suns.

He stopped inches from her boots. She looked up and up and up into hooded dark eyes. Empty, cold, they raked down her body. Horrific stories of crimes committed by Dragath25 prisoners clawed through her mind. Her fingers clenched the dirt, ready to fling. It wasn't much, but she wasn't going down without a fight.

Then he stepped past, his laser-like gaze finding a new target in the twisted metal behind her.

Her gaze swung to Davies'.

The same mix of panic and confusion was clear on her fellow trainee's face. *What the hell?* she mouthed.

Bella shrugged. Who knew? But she didn't intend to miss an opportunity.

Neither made a sound as Bella shifted under Davies and carefully, quietly, lifted her to standing. As she moved, Bella monitored mud man, who was even now picking through the rubble with purposeful intent. Did he intend to rape and kill them after? Was he hoping they'd run so he'd give chase? She had absolutely no idea, but a single glance at his muscled back, sculpted arms, and solid thighs rammed home that he could easily do whatever he wanted if he got hold of her. She didn't intend to give him that chance.

"Start hopping toward those rocks. Nice and quiet." She whispered the words in Davies' ear as she walked them both backwards. She could only pray there weren't more like mud man right behind.

Her colleague shook her head. "I'm not deserting you again."

Bella cut her off. "I'm coming, too. But if he suddenly turns around and comes after us, I'll split off. Give him something to chase. Get to any cave you can. I'll find you there."

Another eerie shriek split the air, ending their discussion. The terrible cry was joined by another. And another.

Davies' hand clenched round Bella's shoulder. Goosebumps rose on her flesh. The feral sound was like nothing she'd ever heard.

Was it her imagination or did mud man start moving faster? He never looked up, simply strode through the wreckage, tossing pieces left and right, stepping over the dead without even a hesitation.

Taking the hint, she moved faster as well, the increased distance from their unwelcome visitor giving her a bit more confidence. The shrieks seemed to have ended her colleague's resistance, too. Davies wobbled backwards, almost dragging Bella, the wind battering them as debris from the growing storm dug into their flesh.

Bella's gaze flickered to Winthrop now covered in a fine film of dirt. Despite the ominous wind, he remained unmoving on the ground, the erratic rise and fall of his chest the only proof he still lived.

A sense of helpless fury shot through her. He was going to die—horribly, by the sound of whatever was heading their way—and she couldn't think of how to save him. She was barely certain she and Davies were going to come out of this alive.

"We have no choice." Davies' gaze was also locked on their boss.

"I know."

They were almost to the rocks when mud man gave a grunt, yanked something from the wreckage, and tucked it into a pack slung across his back. He swiveled back around, his gaze landing unerringly on them.

Bella's breath caught. Her legs turning to water.

He jogged toward them while she pulled Davies along. Her colleague chanted *oh no, oh no, oh no,* and Bella's heart pounded against her ribs and she wanted to scream to the sky with outrage and—

He passed by them so close she felt the heat of his big body brush against her shoulder. Then she was looking at his back as muscles rippled and he heaved himself up the rock face like some kind of flipping mountain goat, leaving them behind sucking in dirt.

"Wait!" The word popped out before she fully thought it through.

"Bella, no," hissed Davies.

But it was too late. As if Bella's words were law, mud man froze on the ledge above.

She took a deep breath. "Help us. Please."

He didn't move.

"We won't make it otherwise." The truth tasted bitter in the back of her throat.

"Bella, don't—"

"Please." Bella pleaded, ignoring Davies. She thought of her sister and brother. Of how quickly they'd be removed from Council protection if she didn't make it back to Earth. "I'll...I'll do whatever you want if you'll only help us."

He landed in a crouch at her boots.

Every frantic heartbeat felt like a hundred years as he unfolded to standing, at least a full head and a half taller, his breath a warm puff against her forehead. So close she could see the bump where his nose had been broken. So close she could see long, thick lashes and the rim of deep, dark blue that gave his eyes their inky black color. So close she could see the sharp blades of jaw and cheekbones that produced his fearsome scowl.

She took a protective step back.

Rough hands encircled her forearms, checking her in place. "Anything?" His voice was a low, rusty rumble.

Bella dug deep for courage, her gaze locking with bottomless black. "Anything."

CHAPTER THREE

Bella helped Davies slide down the rock wall and then dropped to the ground herself, her breathing a near wheeze. Their near-sprint up the rocky cliff trail while battered by howling dry winds had drawn on her last reserves. But even her loud panting and the whirling dust storm wasn't enough to drown out the shrieks far below.

A shudder ran through her. Whoever was down there had made it to the wreckage. Next to her, Davies slammed her hands over her ears, her body rocking to and fro.

Bella barely resisted doing the same. The frenzied screeching and cracking of the shuttle being torn to bits was terrifying to hear. Even knowing she and her colleagues were deep in the hidden cave and the storm would cover their tracks didn't help. She could only pray the shuttle explosion had brought a quick death to the crew she hadn't been able to save.

Not even breathing hard, mud man laid a still unconscious Winthrop by her feet.

Their gazes locked.

"Thank you." She meant it, too. Without him, they'd never have made it this far. He'd found a metal bar among the wreckage and twisted it so Davies could use it as a cane. He slung Winthrop over his shoulder more gently than she would have expected and scrambled up the cliffs with ease, his astonishing array of muscles shifting and flexing as he moved.

"Come." He held out a calloused palm.

She swallowed hard, her stare raking from his scowling face to his wide chest and muscular thighs. Payment had already come due.

"No." Davies grabbed Bella's arm, glaring at the mud man. "This isn't right. Take me instead."

His scowl deepened.

"It's okay." Bella hurriedly slid her hand into his. Davies' offer was unbelievably brave, but Bella would never allow it. Her colleague was Council—and injured. She'd never survive this. Plus, the idea of a deal had been Bella's from the start. And she couldn't regret it. Not when they were all still alive.

His skin was rough—and surprisingly warm.

A shiver slid down her spine. So much so that it took her a second to realize he'd gone perfectly still. His gaze locked on their intertwined palms. Something that looked a lot like wonder etched in the hard planes of his face.

Her gaze skittered to Davies'. Her colleague looked equally confused.

It hit Bella then. Human contact. He was reacting to the sensation of touch. Cherishing something as simple as the heat of her palm against his.

A wave of sympathy rippled through her. This man might be a criminal, but he was also a living being. One who had clearly been alone for a very long time.

On instinct, she interlaced her fingers with his, pressing their hands closer.

He shuddered, his eyes sinking shut, his face tilting upward, the way a person might delight in the sun on his face after a hard, dark winter. Her chest went tight.

After a lifetime of being just one more mouth to feed, one more body that had to be clothed and housed using Earth's ever dwindling resources, the feeling of mattering to someone was unfamiliar—and nice.

"It's okay." It was the same words she'd said before, but this time she meant it. "We're on your side....F—friends."

His eyes flared open, his grip tightening, more possessive now than cherishing. All hints of vulnerability wiped away. "I'm not looking for a friend."

He pulled her to stand on shaky legs, his voice a rusty, husky growl, as if he hadn't used it much. Their bodies so close, the heat of his skin scorched her own.

Standing inches apart, she felt even smaller, the top of her head barely level with his chest. She tried to hold onto the image of wonder she'd seen on his face, but it wouldn't stay. Now, he just looked dangerous—and hungry. *I'm not looking for a friend.* Not a promising beginning.

Against her will, her gaze dropped to the loincloth that did little to hide the rising evidence of his desire. Her stomach spasmed. Mud man was looking to be as big and thick there as he was everywhere else.

His hand contracted around hers.

Her head snapped up.

"Your deal. Your choice." He released his hold, a message all its own.

Her mouth went dry. She understood. He wouldn't force her. She'd been the one to suggest the trade. It was up to her to choose what happened next.

Not exactly what she'd expected from a Dragath25 criminal, but the same could be said of most everything he'd done thus far.

Her gaze flickered to Davies, to Winthrop, to the cave opening where even now those unholy shrieks rattled through the unguarded entrance. But she didn't stop there. She took in the metal crutch at Davies' side. Recalled the careful way Winthrop had been laid to the ground. The look on his face when she'd slid her palm against his.

She cleared her throat. "You fulfill your part of the deal. I'll do what you want."

His nostrils flared. Without another word, he wrapped his hand around her wrist and half dragged, half guided her deeper into the cave.

She heard Davies' pained gasp as she tried to stand and shuffle after them—and Bella truly appreciated the woman's continued willingness to fight for her, but there was nothing Davies could do. Nothing any of them could do.

He was big and strong enough to have taken her without giving anything in return. That he hadn't simply used brute force, that he'd asked, that he'd been willing to walk away, said something. But pissing him off couldn't be wise. One call and those shrieking beasts below would be aware of their presence.

They might be secure for now, but mud man still held their lives in his hands.

"Davies, please. I'll be fine. Look after Dr. Winthrop." She called the words over her shoulder, her voice surprisingly steady.

Whatever her colleague said was swallowed up as mud man hustled Bella through the twists and turns of the narrow cave. With every hurried step deeper into the bowels of the cliff, Bella's calm eroded. If he wanted to hurt her, he could. If he wanted to torment her and then kill her, he could.

It was almost impossible to comprehend that this was really happening. That this morning she'd woken up in her own neat cot in the women's quarters of the Academy research shuttle, a junior researcher with moderate hopes for literally saving the world, and now she was about to be taken and god knows what else on a hard cave floor by a criminal with cold, dark eyes.

She couldn't get pregnant or catch some horrible disease thanks to the yearly shot required of all Council Academy scientific and military personnel, but such precautions couldn't protect her from anything else.

Her muscles twitched with the urge to resist, to take a surprise swing and flee before he understood what was happening, but such an act was beyond foolish. Mud man was too strong. Too powerful. Too dangerous. She'd likely be badly hurt if she tried to fight him.

As if he knew her thoughts, mud man's grip tightened and he pulled until she was pressed flat against his side.

She muffled a gasp.

He heard it anyway. Dark brows narrowed over midnight eyes as his gaze slipped to where his hand circled her wrist. His hold loosened.

"It narrows ahead. Stay close or you'll get cut."

Bella blinked stupidly. His voice was a dark, smoky rumble that rolled down her spine and, under different circumstances, would have sent her senses skittering. Now, it just confused her. Was he…was he truly trying to prevent her from getting hurt?

Before she could think how to ask, he was moving forward again, her wrist still unquestionably encircled in his grasp, her body held tight against his as the cave walls narrowed and the path in front of them grew dark. So close his earthy, male scent invaded her lungs, far more appealing than she would have expected given the dirt covering every inch of him. So close the rough prickle of mud abraded her left arm where skin rather than shirt pressed against his side.

Her shirt grew damp. The air hotter. Then, without warning, they turned a sharp corner, and halted.

Her head snapped up, a sharp breath strangling in her throat at the shocking sight only a few feet ahead.

Awe whispered through her.

Beams of hazy sunlight from small cracks in the cave illuminated a vivid turquoise body of water. It glistened like a jewel while emerald colored plants with large, compound, fan-like leaves crowded along the banks. Palms. Actual thriving, gorgeous healthy palms. From the Arecaceae family, if she wasn't mistaken, though they didn't have the same unbranched stem as the one's in her study guides. Delicate purple fruit sprouted from their split trunks. And the smell…she drew in a deep breath, her nose twitching at the strange, wonderful scent. Floral. Rich. Alive.

Nothing like this had existed on Earth for centuries. But here...her heart leapt. Winthrop had been right. Maybe there was hope for Earth, after all.

She skipped forward. Only to be brought up short by an unmovable leash around her wrist. Her gaze clashed with hungry, dark eyes.

"Take off your clothes."

Her euphoria crashed and burned. For a brief instance, she'd forgotten.

But with every second that mud man loomed above her, his dark eyes boring into her, watching, waiting, his jaw tight, his muscles rigid, the reality of what awaited built inside.

"I won't force you." His words were a growl, but their meaning came through loud and clear nonetheless. He was again offering her a way out.

Her breath shuddered in and out.

She could turn back now. She could renege on the deal. It looked like he'd actually let her walk away. But without his help, she, Davies, and Winthrop would never make it until the search and rescue team arrived. No one would ever know what she'd found here today.

Her gaze shifted to the fan-like plants. Now she had yet another reason to survive this, she told herself. This place. These plants. They could be the key to saving her sister and brother.

As quick as the thought came, she shut out the memory of her sweet siblings' faces. She didn't want them connected in any way with what was about to happen.

"My choice." Awkwardly, she unsealed the top portion of her uniform, her shaking fingers making it difficult. Beside her, mud man had gone disturbingly still.

It wasn't as if she hadn't had sex just for the sake of sex before, she reminded herself. Long hours of studying and work and scraping by hadn't allowed for anything more than the few quick, clumsy joinings with barrack mates to scratch an itch. Sure, she'd known them longer than five minutes and none had been criminals, but there'd been no emotional connection.

Today was just more of the same. At least that's what she tried to tell herself.

When the seal reached its end at her bellybutton, she took a deep breath and let the dirt-covered uniform slide from her arms before pushing it off her hips in one fell swoop. It crumpled to the ground around her feet, leaving her in nothing but her white bra and panties. Her skin prickled at the exposure, her nipples crinkling into tight buds as the cooler air hit her body.

A choked curse had her gaze flying to his.

What she saw made her heart beat even faster. No longer cold, no longer empty, mud man's dark stare glittered with raw hunger as it roamed her breasts and belly and thighs. The wonder was back, too. The dark blue rim she'd noticed before expanding so wide it nearly swallowed the black.

Her arms instinctively moved to cover herself.

"Take off the rest." The rough command had her hands dropping back to her sides.

With jerky movements, she kicked off her boots. Then, she unclasped her bra in one efficient move and let it drop to the ground before pushing her panties down her hips and stepping out of those as well. There. She'd done it.

She forced herself to keep her arms by her sides. *For survival. For survival.* She chanted the words over and over to herself.

Seconds ticked by. Nothing happened. The only sounds in the cave were the rhythmic drip of water and the erratic scrape of her breath sawing in and out.

Her stare flickered to his.

"Beautiful." His single rasped word surprised her. So, too, did the intensity of his dark gaze.

His hands fisted at his side. More seconds ticked by. Still, he made no move to grab her. Simply stared as if memorizing every inch. Unsure, she shifted on her bare feet, a flush of heat warming her cheeks and her chest. The wonder in his gaze making her throat go tight all over again as it had with their first touch.

"Go into the water." His voice was deeper than before.

She started, confused. She'd expected him to be on her already.

"You've got his blood all over you." He sounded almost accusatory. "Go."

She wanted to ask why the hell it mattered, but his hands were already unwinding the cloth at his hips.

Turning fast, she headed to the water, uncaring that the temperature was slightly cooler than expected, barely registering the unfamiliar oily sensation of the water clinging to her skin. Wading toward the deeper middle, she sunk beneath the surface to her shoulders, the transparent film giving her little protection, but somehow calming her just the same.

A splash sounded. Powerful ripples washed against her back like a surging tide. He'd entered the water. He was coming for her.

The coward in her wanted to stay where she was, eyes slammed shut. The officer in her knew she had to turn and face this head on.

She whirled and discovered only small bubbles on the surface of the water. An inky cloud of red and brown streamed in all directions followed by foamy white. Then a dark head broke the surface and he was standing before her, waist high in the water, a mud man no more.

Her mouth opened on a tiny *o*.

Without the dirt, dark, thick hair shorn close to his scalp was now visible along with olive skin, a wide forehead, low brows, firm lips, and a square jaw. Tiny droplets left his long lashes spikey while rivulets of water tracked over chiseled cheekbones, down his sculpted chest and abdomen, to a small trail of dark hair that snaked from his belly button to disappear into the water. Scars of various length and width tracked across miles of pure, hard muscle.

My *God*, mud man was a flesh and blood man—an incredibly masculine one. If she'd met him at the Academy or the barracks on Earth, she would have been unable to stop staring. He was that beautiful.

Then his hand shot out and her daze shattered.

With a hiss, she stumbled back a step.

One dark eyebrow rose. "Here."

She looked down to see a small white bar in his hand.

"It's soap." His tone was brusque. "The drones dump trash from Earth. Use it."

It was another long speech. This one seemed to come easier. Like his vocal chords were warming up. Like he was remembering how to actually talk to someone else. But beyond that, she had no idea what was going on here. Why he was taking the time to give her soap. Clean her up.

She hated not being able to read him at all. She hated not knowing if the brief flashes of humanity she'd seen in his gaze were real or not.

"Thank you." It took all her courage to reach out and take the bar from his hand, the brush of her fingertips against his rough palm sending adrenaline surging through her. But when he remained still, when he allowed her to draw back her hand, soap clutched tight, her heartbeat slowed to something just below painful. "I—I've never used one before. The Academy only allows lasers for cleaning. The use of water was banned a long time ago." She stopped short.

Of course, he knew that. He wasn't from some distant galaxy. He was from Earth. He just wasn't welcome there anymore.

His lips flat lined. "I've been here a while, but not as long as that."

Was that a joke? His expression offered no clue.

"Of course." Hands shaking, she took the soap and rubbed it against her arm. The blood stayed put. She rubbed harder.

She hadn't expected this...this talking. Or the kindness of a bath—with soap. It was confusing.

"You need the water to make it work." Rough hands reached out and took the soap, dunking it under the water, making that same foamy circle she'd seen before.

"Turn around." His voice had gone husky again.

That overworked heart of hers started up double time once again. Her feet remained planted where they were.

He waited for longer than she would have expected before he spoke again, his jaw locked tight. "Anything?" It was a reminder. A reproach. A challenge.

And her last chance to change her mind.

Her eyes sunk shut. *I can do this. I need to do this.*

She whirled around, bracing for a grab. A strike. But the deliberate slow glide of a calloused fingertip down the bumps of her spine slammed through her with more force than any blow.

CHAPTER FOUR

"Pull your hair to one side." 673's voice was gruffer than intended, but staying in control was taking all his effort. The creature he'd become roared at him to throw her down and ram inside. To take what was his. The Dragath25 way.

And he could. He could do whatever he wanted with her. His strength gave him that right. Her defenselessness made her easy prey. There were no rules here on Dragath25. No honor. Only violence and might.

But he didn't throw her down. He didn't ram inside. The feel of soft silk beneath his fingertip too good to rush. Hazy memories of the man he'd once been whispered that the smells and the sighs and the hot little mewling sounds of a woman on the edge were worth the wait.

That even a bit of the man he'd been still existed confused him almost as much as it angered him. But all of that was secondary to the feel of her smooth skin as he dragged his fingertip down her spine.

She'd stayed. He'd thought several times she wouldn't. He'd braced himself for the reversal. Lectured the man he'd once been to damn well walk away before he became even more of a monster. But she'd surprised him. And he wasn't about to lose the chance to experience something he'd never thought to feel again.

He leaned forward, skimming his nose just above the smooth line of her shoulder. Holy hell. The scent of her...of woman. Of light. Of softness. The faint hint of vanilla still clinging to her skin.

The soap cracked in his palm.

It was a good reminder. Control was essential. Control was imperative or the fragile, trembling woman before him would turn to dust in his hands. Like everything else he'd ever had.

He'd told her to turn around because the sight of her body—of all that creamy white skin, full lush breasts tipped by perfect pink nipples, hourglass curves, and bare, mouthwatering mound—had made going slow impossible. But even with her back to him he was in trouble. That ass....it called to him even now.

He leaned in close. "You smell...good."

She started. Then seemed to force herself to relax. "That's hard to imagine, but thanks." Her voice had a high-pitched forced nonchalance he didn't like as much as the one she used when bossing that bastard soldier around. "I'm covered in soot and dirt and dust. Even my hair must stink."

His gaze shifted to her hair. He hadn't really paid attention beyond noting it was long and wavy and feminine enough to check off each of his boxes. But now he was curious. Finding a layer of control he hadn't even known he possessed, he shoved back at the lust riding him hard. "Go under."

There was a momentary hesitation and then, on a deep breath, she sank under. Instantly, her hair fanned out in all directions, tangled silk. Fumbling—his hands seeming too big and awkward for the first time—he grabbed for the strands as gently as possible, letting the soap skim through them and over her pink scalp. Inky grey clouds slid from her hair, revealing a golden brown he was pretty sure would turn to yellow gold when dry. His fighter girl was a blonde.

For some reason, it brought relief. His wife had been a brunette.

He gave the woman's hair a gentle tug. Understanding, she emerged from the water, wiping her eyes.

Done with waiting, he kept his fist wrapped around her hair, walking backwards until they were standing only up to her thighs in the shallow water, guiding her closer and closer, ignoring her little gasp of dismay and the stiffness of her posture, until her perfect backside pressed against his front.

A groan strangled in his throat. The warm press of her soft, wet skin, and the feel of his throbbing cock nestling in the crease of her ass was better than anything he could have imagined.

Except for that first touch....the heat of her small palm pressed against his, her fingers voluntarily lacing with his....God, that had almost brought him to his knees.

After the first few years on Dragath25, pain hadn't been as big a part of his day. Life had settled into one numb, bleak cycle after another. But pleasure...he'd thought that sensation gone for good.

Until she offered him anything.

Her body trembled as he slid his hands across the silk of her creamy shoulders, down her arms, the foam from the soap leaving streaks of white. Tracing the softness of her warm flesh ecstasy and hell.

He sucked down a shuddering breath, scrambling for an anchor, drowning in sensation. After eight years of a bleak void, the awakening of every nerve ending was almost painful. The shocking riot of another's scent and touch and sound almost too acute to bear. And still he couldn't make himself stop.

She was so tiny his palms easily spanned her back. Yet she'd taken on soldier bastard and him. And done whatever was necessary to save her friends. Maybe she had the kind of strength necessary to survive Dragath25. At least longer than most females.

"Do you want to know my name?"

His hands stilled. He should have known his fighter girl wouldn't go down quietly.

Her voice was part whisper, part reproach. "It's Cadet Annabella West. Bella, for short."

"It suits." *But I prefer fighter girl.*

His hands glided to her full tits, rolling her sweet pink nipples between thumb and forefinger. So smooth. So stiff. Her sharp gasp only made his dick throb harder.

"I came here on a mission." Her voice was growing less steady, more breathy with every second he played with her breasts. "I came to find a way to save Earth. To—"

He splayed his hand down her flat belly and cupped her mound. "Fighter girl?"

"Yes?" Her word was an unsteady hiss.

"Shut up." He nipped at her throat, his fingers ghosting over the soft folds of her pussy. Getting her used to his touch. Reminding her what was to come. She wasn't wet. He hadn't expected her to be. There were things that needed to be established first. Things her mind needed to accept before her body followed.

"What was doesn't matter. The past is over." Another inmate had told him the same thing early in his arrival. When he'd still been clinging to the man he was. To the life and the rules and the norms he'd known on Earth. The lesson had saved his life. "Life on Dragath25 is short. Ugly. Brutal. Every day you survive is a miracle."

He paused, letting the words sink in. "Do you understand what I'm saying, female?" She nodded, but he pushed himself to continue anyway. He'd been out of the habit of talking for a while, but this was important. He needed her to understand. "This is about pleasure. Not pain. I don't get off on pain."

She stilled, and he thought he heard a small sob. It caused an odd tightness in his chest. He should have mentioned no pain before. He was definitely out of practice.

"I won't hurt you." His thumb skimmed over her clit, gently, barely there. "On Dragath25, you take your pleasure where you can, when you can. Because tomorrow you might not be alive to feel anything at all."

There was a moment of silence, the only sound the rasp of her too fast breaths, and then, to his immense satisfaction, she relaxed a fraction against him, her legs widening ever so slightly to accommodate his touch. "No pain is good. I...I can do that."

Her courage hit him like a sucker punch. Stealing his breath, sending his limbs twitching, his blood roaring in his veins, his body demanding its due, while his mind screamed at him to get the hell out of this cave before it was too late. To turn tail and run before her fearlessness turned this into something he'd never intended.

For eight years, he hadn't given a damn about another soul. It had kept him sane. It had kept him alive. Feeling something for this woman besides lust wasn't a part of the plan.

But before he could make good on his thoughts, her hand closed over his, anchoring him to her, her fingers lacing with his just as she had the first time he'd touched her. "It's okay."

Fuck. She was comforting him. Soothing him like she might a wild animal, which proved just how insightful she was.

He wanted to shake off her touch. To tell her he didn't need a damn thing from anyone, but there was no way. Not when his breath was shuddering in and out. Not when he couldn't have moved his hand even if 225's entire pack suddenly descended.

No! This was about scratching an itch. Seizing the moment. Nothing else.

Determined, he forced his body to stillness. Moved his palms down her legs, noting the way she shivered, noting the small catch in the back of her throat as he brushed behind her knees, the back of her thighs. The way her breath shuddered when he ran his fingertips along the crease of her ass. How her body quivered when his hand cupped her throat, his mouth sucking on the vulnerable tendon he'd exposed. His lust ramping higher with every touch.

He got the distinct sense his fighter girl liked things on the edge.

Just a little longer came the pained chant in his mind as his hands glided over her soft skin, learning her, relearning himself, sweat beading on his back and every muscle tightening to the point of pain as he forced himself to go slow.

Then, finally, thankfully, her muscles lost the last of their tenseness, her thighs parting in surrender as his fingers worked her pussy—sliding through hot-as-hell wetness that only made him harder. She was wet. And hot. And a million times more erotic than any dream he'd had these last lonely years.

He needed more. More sensation. More touch. More her.

"Hold on." Without warning, he turned her in his arms. Lifted her up so she had no choice but to lock her ankles behind his ass. And waded toward the bank.

Hands no longer shaking, he laid her on the soft moss. Her legs slipped from his waist. He stepped between them, forcing them wide. The sight of her spread beneath him made him groan.

Her eyes grew three sizes, trepidation and uncertainty—but no longer terror—flitting through their gorgeous green depths. Emerald green. Like the plants around him. He hadn't noticed that before.

"What are you planning to—"

He swooped in and latched onto her pretty pink pussy before she could finish her question. His action was answer enough. He'd forgotten the mouthwatering tangy taste, the exotic scent, the unbelievable feel. And his fighter girl....she tasted better than anything he remembered. Especially when she gave a little mewling cry and opened her legs wider, letting him in. Taking pleasure where she could. Proving herself a true survivor.

The last of his control snapped.

On a roar, he reared up, his hands wrapping around her thighs, lifting her lower body off the ground and lining her up with his dick. Their gazes locked as he rubbed against her once, twice, using her juice as lubrication. "I'm coming inside." It was a declaration.

"I know." She panted beneath him, her gaze clear. Steady. A clear sign she wasn't as lost in her pleasure as she should be, but there was a flush on her cheeks and her pretty pink slit was swollen and wet. It would have to be enough.

"Touch yourself. Make it good." He shook his head, fighting for control.

She was still for an instant and then understanding and determination settled in her gaze, outweighing shame or embarrassment or fear. Watching her fingers slide into her soft folds almost drove him back to his knees.

Shaking with need, his gaze locked on her hand, he worked himself inside, one slow fucking inch at a time. Her tight hole making it impossible for him to do more than thrust slowly. Her growing moans of pleasure whipping his desire into a greater frenzy. Until he was buried completely. So deep, his balls smacked against her ass. And, oh holy fuck, the feel of her was unbelievable.

He pumped harder. Faster. His hips moving at near desperate speed, chasing the kind of satisfaction he'd never thought to feel again. Driven to the brink by the hot as hell movement of her fingers circling her clit harder and faster, frantic now as her gaze grew heavy lidded and he rammed deep inside her.

Connected. With another human being. As he'd never expected to be again.

"Anything. You remember, female?" His words were a near growl. "You said anything and I want it. I want you to come for me."

As if waiting for his command, she broke apart, her body shuddering as her fingers went wild and her cunt clenched down on his dick, milking him so hard and deep it threw him into his own orgasm, his back bowing as wave after wave of pleasure slammed through him, making it damn near impossible to stand—and still he kept thrusting, never wanting it to end—until every last bit of satisfaction was wrung from him.

Holy shit. He almost felt...at peace.

Until he remembered this was Dragath25. And here, after the pleasure, there was always pain.

The man's sudden tensing nudged Bella from her breathless stupor. The aftershocks of her orgasm were still coursing through her body, his thick cock deep inside her, her legs spread wide, her bottom still lifted off the ground.

Their gazes fused. He looked almost wary. Wasn't that supposed to be her role?

Maybe he couldn't see it, but the strongest emotions pulsing through her right then were gratitude and pride...and the ache of a woman well pleasured.

The way he'd looked at her...the way he'd handled her...as if she were something precious....as if simply touching her was something extraordinary...it wasn't something she'd experienced before.

She'd seen people look at faded pictures of the lost forests like that, but other people? In a world where people like her—people without parents or Council influence—were forced to sleep stacked atop one another and crammed shoulder to shoulder in crowded eating halls for a few synthetic, flavorless scraps of condensed food, touch was taken for granted, viewed more as a necessity to be suffered than a pleasure. But with him, it hadn't felt like that at all. *She* hadn't felt like just another burden. She'd felt...she'd felt like she mattered.

This stranger—this criminal—could have hurt her. Instead, he'd demanded her pleasure and given her the tools to find her own. And she'd risen to the challenge. Taken something that could have been hell and made it heaven. Maybe it wouldn't make sense to everyone, but she'd done what she'd had to do and ended up having the best sex of her life.

"What's your name?" She needed to know.

He froze. It almost seemed like he flinched.

The silence stretched.

Her high vanished. "Never mind. It's not important."

"673."

"That's not a name." She kept her tone light, unchallenging. She wasn't a fool. She understood fucking her hadn't suddenly made her special. But they'd made some sort of connection, damn it.

His scowl deepened. "It is here on Dragath25."

"But you had a name back on Earth."

His hands landed on either side of her head with a thump. His fingers steady. No tremor, no trace of vulnerability to be seen. "This isn't Earth, fighter girl. Trying to pretend otherwise won't help either of us."

Her gaze searched his for any sign of the softness she was almost certain had been there before. Nothing.

Had she imagined the connection to begin with? Attributed more humanity to him than was there to make the whole exchange more palatable? "This may not be Earth, but we're still human beings. That doesn't change."

"You're wrong." His hard body blanketed her as he drove deep, making her gasp. "On Dragath25, there are no names. No humanity." He thrust deeper. "No selflessness." Another thrust. "And definitely no happy ever-after." His fingers tangled in her hair, restraining her so she couldn't look away even if she wanted. "If you want to stay alive, you accept that now."

She nodded slowly, carefully. The small tug at her scalp combined with the friction of his thick cock made it hard to concentrate on his words. But the bleakness in his tone came through loud and clear. As did his message.

Trying to gentle him with reminders of Earth wouldn't work. Imagining he'd felt anything like what she had would only bring trouble. And whatever vulnerability, whatever humanity, she might have awakened with her touch had been erased as if it never existed.

"I—I understand."

"You want me to keep you and those two safe?" he challenged. "The woman and that dying Council Officer?"

"He's not going to die, damn it." The fiercely spoken words flew from her before she could think better of it.

673 stilled, his eyes narrowing. "Is he your man?"

The air was suddenly thick with danger.

"Dr. Winthrop? No. He's my superior. Nothing more."

The hold on her hair loosened. "Good. Because I don't share." He started moving inside her again, his hand slipping between them to rub her already sensitive clit. "As long as you understand what you and I have going on here and what it will take to keep them alive, we'll be fine."

"Oh, God." Pleasure surged through her, her eyelids sinking shut. Her arms stretching above her head as her back arched to better meet his thrust. It was so much easier to lose herself in the moment than think about what he was demanding—and deliberately holding back. Until a hard tug on her hair had her eyelids springing open, denying her oblivion.

"Not yet, female." His dark gaze bore into her, his fingers stilling against her clit in a deliberate bid for control. "I want this clear. You use me for protection. I use you for pleasure. That's the deal you offered. That's the deal I'm accepting. Simple as that."

She forced herself to concentrate. "Agreed." There was no choice. No point either in acknowledging that small stab of disappointment. She didn't need to feel special. Or exchange names. Or see wonder in his gaze. All she needed was for him to keep to their agreement.

It wasn't as if this deal was indefinite anyway. Rescuers would be coming. She needed only to appease him for the short-term.

As if he sensed her underlying rebellion, he pushed further. "You do what I say, when I say it. Dragath25 is not an easy place to survive."

She swallowed hard. "And Cadet Davies? Will you leave her alone?"

"The injured female?" He frowned. "I've no interest in her as long as you're around."

Not exactly sweet nothings, but it would have to do.

"Th–then, yes, I understand. I agree. Anything. When you say it. As long as you keep us safe."

"Good girl." His fingers worked her faster now, his thrusts harder. Tremors radiated from her pussy to her toes and up her spine. His hold on her hair tightening once again as he exposed her throat, his teeth grazing the line of her neck until his lips closed over her ear.

The vulnerability of her position sent a different kind of tremor rushing through her.

"And fighter girl? You want to call me something other than 673? Call me Convict. Because from here on out," he whispered, his breath a warm rasp against her ear, "that's who owns your ass."

CHAPTER FIVE

Bella came awake a few deep breaths at a time. Had something made a sound? She stifled a moan, her body protesting even that subtle movement. Convict had taken her more times than she could count and made her come even more than that.

She'd never seen that look of wonder again, but there'd been a desperate quality to his touch, as if he thought she might disappear any second. He'd been relentless, fierce, his hands and mouth on every part of her—except her mouth. He'd never once kissed her.

Rolling onto her side, she scanned the room. She was alone. Not that she hadn't already known it. After hours of having him above her, inside her, behind her—his scent and power seeping into her very pores, his hands and mouth marking every part of her—she was acutely attuned to the man.

A tremor of panic settled in her gut. Had he deserted them already? Gotten what he wanted and taken off?

She was scrambling to her knees when she saw a pile of neatly folded clothes near where her head had been. Her dirty uniform was nowhere in sight.

Her heart slowed. He wouldn't leave clothes if he wasn't keeping his word, right?

Moving toward the pile, she cocked her head, listening, unsure if the rocky cavern was playing tricks on her. Had she just heard another odd noise? The same kind that had woken her from sleep?

Only the slow drip of water echoed back at her. She dismissed it as nerves and kept moving. Convict hadn't given her any instructions so she could only hope doing what she liked wouldn't anger him. She had so many questions. About the cave. How he'd found it. If he lived here. About the clothes. Who'd made those terrifying shrieks? But he clearly hadn't been in the mood for conversation the last couple of hours. She got the unfortunate sense he might never be.

The clothes were surprisingly soft, and though way too big, she was able to roll the pants up underneath the large long sleeve shirt. It took her a while of fumbling to figure out the closure mechanism. The latest Command Council Earth suits were made of rough synthetic material and affixed with magnetic bonds that required only a finger pad along the seam to close. Like the soap, the clothes Convict had left were likely old toss offs from Earth. But they were warm and clean and a lot better than her bloody uniform. It didn't escape her notice he hadn't left her bra or underwear. Thankfully, her boots were still there.

Once dressed, the vibrant plants drew her eye, but she forced herself past. Of primary importance was checking on Davies and Winthrop. She needed to make sure they were okay. Plus, after a lifetime spent under Command Council protocol accounting for her movements with hourly productivity reports, it was disorienting to be suddenly so unregulated. Though meeting Davies' knowing gaze wouldn't be easy, she'd just have to brave it out. Like Convict had said, different rules for Dragath25. Cadet Davies would have to understand and—

A low hiss reverberated through the passageway. Eerie. Inhuman.

Bella was running before the noise came to a silent, abrupt end.

"Stay back!" Convict's furious command had Bella skidding to a halt.

Her breath strangled in her throat.

Davies cowered against the far cave wall, an unconscious Winthrop and a spilled bucket of water at her feet. Convict, dressed only in his loincloth and boots, a bleeding claw mark on his bare chest, stood in front of them. His legs braced wide apart, a large spear in one hand.

Only three arms lengths away stood an eight-foot tall, hissing, four-legged beast with huge claws. Even bigger fangs. And a striped muscular hide that looked like it would easily break the spindly piece of wood in Convict's hand.

A musky, rank odor permeated the cave. Bella's primitive intuition recognized it as the scent of an animal, but she had no way to confirm. Earth animals had died out long ago.

Determined not to panic, she scanned the space for some kind of weapon. A sharp rock? An even sharper stick? *Damn Pogue and those other soldiers.* If they'd left her a gun, she could at least have given them a chance against this creature.

Swooping down to grab a few loose nearby rocks, she took a cautious step toward the beast's other side.

"I told you to stay back." Convict's low hiss made the animal's ears flatten farther. "Get to the water. They won't go near it."

Ignoring him, she took another careful step. "I'm not leaving my colleagues here. If I can get around it, I'll distract it while you take them to safety."

"No." Convict's refusal was absolute.

She took another step anyway, dirt from the rocks sticking uncomfortably to her sweaty palm "How fast can this thing run?"

"Tigos are too fast. You'll never outrun one. Get. Back. Now."

The tone of his voice had her wondering if she should be more afraid of him or the beast. "I can help."

"I don't need it."

Then before she could disagree, Convict leapt forward, he and his spear soaring straight for the tigos' vicious fangs.

The creature's paws swiped forward, its mouth opening wide.

She was already running forward, a scream on her lips, when Convict flipped, dodging the tigos' claw. He slid to a halt beneath the beast. In the next heartbeat, his spear shot upward, piercing the creature's vulnerable belly.

Hit, the creature reared back, letting loose a terrible, piercing scream. On an answering roar, Convict seized the end of the spear, jerking it out of the creature's belly. Blood splattered onto the cave floor. It's sickly sweet smell made Bella's stomach jolt.

Convict raised his arm to pierce again.

But the animal was already backpedaling, slamming against the cave wall—barely missing her—before it turned and raced outside.

Resounding silence filled the cavern.

Bella leaned an arm against the cave wall, her knees weak. *Thank God for Convict. That had been too damn close.*

Then something clattered to the ground, and before Bella could turn, rough hands seized her shoulders and whisked her around. Convict stared down at her with dangerous, dark eyes. "I told you to get back."

She ignored the tendril of fear winding up her spine. "I wanted to help."

His hold tightened. "You said you would listen. Don't you know how easy it is to die out here?"

"I'm beginning to understand all too well, but—"

"You broke our deal." He dropped his arms as if he couldn't stand to touch her.

Relief whispered through her. He'd looked so fierce. She half-expected to share the fate of the tigos.

Instead, he seized his spear and stalked to his dirt-colored pack.

Her gaze shifted to Davies, huddled against the wall, guarding Winthrop. Davies was pale, her expression worried, but her face was no longer streaked with soot and a new bandage surrounded her leg. All in all, she looked better than when Bella had seen her last.

Winthrop, too, looked better, though he was clearly still unconscious. His face had been cleaned and there was a wrap around his chest that hadn't been there before.

Convict had been busy while she'd slept.

"You've got about a half an hour."

Bella's gaze flew to the entrance of the cave.

Convict stood in the opening, his back to them. Not even turning around, he slung the backpack over his shoulder. "I left another shirt you can use for bandages and a few bars, but I'd eat them on the run. Tigos can scent another's blood. There'll be more coming. That was a tigos male. The females are five times that size and a hundred times more fierce. Not to mention that 225's pack will have heard the fighting. You don't want to be here when they come to investigate."

"Wait." She rushed forward. "Where are you going?"

"Wherever I want." Jaw clenched tight, he stepped through the cave entrance.

"No, please." She hurried after him. "I'm sorry. I didn't mean to make you mad." She raced to keep up, but he bounded over the rocks on his long legs, easily lengthening the distance between them. "Don't go. We'll die here without your help. Please." The last of her plea clogged in her throat as he rounded a bend and disappeared from sight.

He'd left. Fucked her and flat out left without even a hint of hesitation.

"Fine! Go!" She screamed at the spot where he'd been. "I should have known you wouldn't keep to the deal.

You're nothing but a lowlife Dragath25 criminal. Who needs you?"

She was turning back toward the cave when the ground shook. Reeling around, her eyes went wide. Convict was steamrolling toward her, a murderous look on his face.

She'd only just begun to run when powerful arms jerked her back against hard, warm steel. Clawing, kicking, she tried to break free, but it was no use. Caged by one thick arm around her stomach and one tangled in her hair, she was trapped.

"That's right, fighter girl. I am nothing but a lowlife Dragath25 criminal."

He carried her easily over to a large rock, absorbing her blows like she was nothing more than a pesky insect. Her hands were stinging, her hair stuck to her cheek, her breath coming in gasps by the time he shifted her around, sandwiching her between him and a large boulder.

"Stop." She shoved against his chest. It was as unmovable as the rock at her back.

"Criminals don't stop." He fisted her shirt, drawing her onto her tiptoes, bringing her face in line with his. His knee slid between her thighs, forcing them wide. "We take." The hand fisted in her hair jerked her head back while his other hand skimmed down her body. "We violate."

He ran the pad of his finger along the waistband of her rolled up pants. Back and forth. Like the tigos' twitching tail. Danger evident in every deliberate pass of his hand. "We kill."

Heartbeat slamming against her ribs, she tried to fix this. "I—I shouldn't have said what I did. I'm sorry."

"That's right. You shouldn't have said it." He wrapped his wrist tighter in her hair. "Just like you shouldn't have ignored my direct order."

"I understand that now."

It was as if he didn't hear her. "You think it's easy to survive out here. You think this is a joke. You think I made it on this fucking hellhole this long out of sheer luck."

"No."

"I've seen things you wouldn't believe. Done things I can barely stand to think of." Echoes of those horrors stretched tight across his face. "But I've made it here eight years and I don't intend to die now."

Her chest grew tight. She didn't think she could bear even another few days on this place. She couldn't imagine surviving eight years.

"I'm sorry. You're right." She spoke fast, the words spilling from her, more genuine this time. "I wasn't trying to get you killed. I was trying to help. I–I should have listened. And–and I shouldn't have called you a…a lowlife. I was scared and angry. I appreciate all you've done. Hiding us in the cave. Saving us from the tigos. Even the water and bandages you gave my colleagues." She cleared her throat. "You were keeping to the deal. I was the one who screwed up."

He didn't acknowledge her words, but his grip loosened, the tension in his body lessening. "It's easy to die out here."

"But people make it." Her voice shook. "You've made it. I will, too."

He shook his head, something that looked a lot like regret in his gaze. "You're soft. Delicate." The finger that had been so predatory against her skin now felt like a caress. "Keeping you alive will be next to impossible. Even without the added stubbornness."

A new and astonishing idea flooded through her, a live wire of awareness to her brain. Could it be that it wasn't cold-heartedness that had promoted his departure, but the exact opposite? He didn't want to watch her die.

"I'm stronger than you think. I know you don't know me, but I am."

His fingers stilled against her, proof he was listening.

"When the last wave of famine hit Earth, I was fourteen," she continued. "My parents died from the blight within months. Orphaned, alone, everyone said my younger sister and brother and I wouldn't make it another month. But I kept them alive. Stole when I had to. Worked whatever job I could get. Studied every spare moment. All so I could earn the scores that would get me a Council Academy scholarship and my baby sister and brother the right to live off my pension. And that's what I did. And all three of us were doing just fine until I crashed on this planet." She sucked in a deep breath. "I am going to survive this as well. Trust me."

"I don't trust anyone." His hand fanned possessively across her belly while his nose skimmed along her throat. "But you smell good, female. Unlike anything on Dragath25. Taste even better."

After so many hours in his arms, she knew that rasp. Recognized the hunger. Understood too that he was offering her a second chance. Something she suspected he rarely did.

Her body responded, her skin flushing hot while her nipples tightened and her pussy throbbed. "I won't give you any more trouble. Touch me, Con—" she didn't want to call him that. Not anymore. Not after he'd come back despite what she'd hurled at him. He might be a Dragath25 prisoner, but he was also a man. One whom she was coming to believe had retained more of his humanity than he realized. "If you won't tell me your name, I'm going to call you Hero. It fits better."

He froze. "It doesn't fit at all."

"You've saved me and my friends twice already. That makes you a hero."

She thought he'd be pleased.

"A hero doesn't do what I'm about to do," he growled. "Spread your legs."

He likely expected to elicit fear, but all that prickled across her skin was white-hot lust. He hadn't hurt her before. Even when she'd insulted him.

This had to be a test. One she didn't intend to fail.

She did as commanded. Her fingers curling into his shoulders as he yanked her pants down to her thighs. Cool air swirled around her ass.

"Still want to call me Hero?" His thick finger probed her folds, his gaze challenging as his thumb circled her clit. Slowly. Deliberately.

"No." Pleasure shivered through her. What she wanted was to call him by his name. What she wanted was for him to stop pretending he was worse than he was.

"Good." His voice dropped to a low rasp, that thread of wonder back in his voice. "You're wet."

"Yes." Should she be ashamed? Maybe, but with his calloused hands working the part of her that needed him most, she couldn't seem to care. Plus, this was Dragath25. She could make her own rules. Take pleasure while she could. With a man who was a lot more complicated than he wanted her to believe. "I—I like what you do to me."

His nostrils flared, a shudder running through him. She could tell she'd surprised him. For an instant, something very human—something that looked a lot like regret and guilt and need—flashed in his gaze, but it was gone in the next blink. "Take out my dick. Put it inside you."

He was definitely out to prove he was no hero.

But she remembered the way he'd put himself between her colleagues and the tigos. How he'd attacked the creature when he thought it was coming for her. The flash of hope in his gaze when she'd told him she was determined to survive. The fact that despite his anger, he'd come running back.

Fingers trembling, she slid her hands beneath his loincloth, the heat of his skin a brand against her palm as she gripped him. His cock so thick she couldn't make it even halfway around. She stood on tiptoes, tilting her hips forwards, her back against the rock, as she worked to put him inside.

A groan of frustration escaped. He was so big. She was too small. The angle all wrong. All she could do was rub up against him. "I—I can't."

Before she could even finished, powerful arms slid under her ass, lifting her up so their bodies were in perfect alignment. But instead of sinking inside, he held her poised at the tip of his cock, a message all of its own.

Her gaze flew to his.

She wondered if he knew she could see the raw need he was pretending not to feel.

"Tell me," he commanded.

She knew instantly what he meant. "I can't do this on my own. I need you. I do."

"Who?"

She should have known he'd win in this, too. "You. Convict. I need you."

With a grunt of triumph, he guided her onto his cock, working her deeper, inch by inch, until she took all of him. His big hands moving her back and forth so that she was sliding in and out at his whim. Him using her to fuck him senseless. It was the hottest thing she'd ever experienced.

Her body, already so sensitive, tightened with need, tiny tremors whipping through her as her legs bounded wildly, his movements growing faster, jerkier, as his own pleasure built. Needing an anchor, she ran her hands down the slick, muscled plains of his back. Then his mouth was at her ear, "Come for me, fighter girl."

Surrendering, her body shattered into a thousand pieces.

She was still trying to catch her breath when his strong hand gripped her chin and tipped it to meet his bottomless gaze.

"Lowlife Dragath25 criminals have their uses," he all but growled. "Don't forget it."

CHAPTER SIX

"We'll rest here." Convict's declaration sent Bella looking up, her legs rejoicing. She'd been staring down at her feet, forcing one in front of each other for the last hour now.

"Can I help?"

"I've got him."

Of course, he did. Bella watched Convict guide an unconscious Winthrop to the ground. He'd been carrying the man on his back at a near run—along with his spear and that backpack he refused to let out of his sight—over treacherous, rocky terrain for the last four hours. The hot suns beating down on them all the while.

Even so, Bella doubted this stop was for him. He wasn't even breathing hard while every one of her leg muscles was screaming and poor Davies' shirt was soaked, her face pale.

Still, it wouldn't have killed the man to let her help in some small way.

"I'm going to backtrack and cover our trail. I've left some water and the last of the bars." He held out a smooth, small rock with a hole at either end. "Any trouble, blow this." He held out his spear next. "Don't hesitate. Whatever's coming at you won't, either."

She eyed the weapon. "If we have that, what will you use?"

His warning gaze bore into her. "Take it."

Back rigid, she did as requested. He was already almost out of sight, his mouthwatering golden skin bunching and flexing as he sped away, before she realized she should have asked exactly what might be coming at them. But it was too late now.

After a wide, nervous scan of the surrounding rocky landscape, she dropped beside Davies, who was already checking Winthrop's bandage.

Their gazes met then skittered away.

It was the first time they'd had a moment to talk. When she and Convict had returned from their argument, her face flushed, her hair tangled and wild, Convict had done little more than slap a few bar rations into her and Davies' hands, scoop up Winthrop, and bark out a command for them to follow. He'd set such a fast pace, talking had been impossible. She and Davies had exchanged a couple of grim glances, but that was it.

"You okay?" Davies' voice was thin.

"I'm fine." There were far more important matters to discuss than her emotional state. "I don't know where he's taking us, but I'm charting the direction via the suns as best I can. We'll know how to get back to the crash site and the rescuers when the time comes. Until then it's best to stay with him."

"Maybe so, but..."

"Are you worried he'll go after you? He's given his words he won't. Not as long as I'm available."

"Oh, God." Davies stopped pretending to fiddle with Winthrop's bandages, her expression crumpling. "I'm so sorry. I–I hate that you had to do that for us. For me. Because I'm Council and—"

"I didn't do it because you're Council."

Davies shook her head as if refuting the claim. "I shouldn't have let you. I shouldn't have been such a coward."

"No, please." Bella's hand closed over the woman's thin shoulder. Yes, initiating touch with a Council member without permission was a serious breach of protocol, but there was no reason Convict's notion of different rules for Dragath25 couldn't hold true in this respect as well, and Davies appeared to need more comfort than just words. "Don't feel like that. It isn't what you think."

"Don't lie to me. I heard you. I know what he did to you." Davies' eyes sank shut as she leaned in to Bella's touch. "I hate myself for letting it happen. For doing nothing while he hurt you. I–I know what that's like...and now...." Her hands twisted in her lap. "Now I'm letting it happen to you. I'm a terrible coward."

"He didn't hurt me." Embarrassment had a tight grip on Bella's throat. Sorrow, too. *Someone had hurt Davies.* Badly, if the way the woman's hands shook was any indication.

Emboldened, Bella gripped those trembling hands. Surprisingly, they gripped her right back.

"What you heard wasn't pain, it...it was pleasure." Bella took a deep breath and confessed. "He made me feel good. Better than anything I ever felt before. I–I didn't expect it, but there it is."

Davies' shocked gaze didn't help.

"He's not what you think." Bella felt oddly protective.

"He's a Dragath25 prisoner. He's forcing you to have sex with him." Davies' voice cracked at the end.

"He's not forcing me." Bella kept her voice gentle. Her colleague's confession made this conversation even more delicate than she'd expected. "We have a deal. And so far, he's given far more than he's taken."

Davies remained silent.

Bella squeezed the woman's hand. "I'm sorry someone hurt you. Truth be told, I'd like to find the bastard and feed him to a tigos, but my situation isn't the same. He's brusque and rough, but he's not a monster. Even when he's been angry, he hasn't harmed me. And he's already done more for us than Pogue ever did. We're alive because of Convict."

"Convict? Is—is that his name?"

"No, but it's what he's insisting I call him."

One of Davies' eyebrows shot up.

Bella shrugged. "He's been here for eight years. I don't think he likes to remember the man he was."

"Or maybe that man is gone for good," warned her colleague. "Don't hang your hopes on someone who doesn't exist. He couldn't have been a very good person to begin with anyway. Not if he ended up here." Her eyes sank shut. "Don't...don't let yourself be deceived. I—I know I'm not supposed to speak of Council matters, but I thought my fiancé was a good man once. Then he turned me into his personal punching bag." She shook her head, her watery eyes blinking open to survey the barren landscape. "All I wanted was freedom. Look what I got instead."

"This isn't the end." Bella tried to keep the shock from her voice. There was far more to her fellow researcher than she'd ever realized. And far less to her foolish presumption that being part of an elite Council family line meant an end to all worries. "You can still have that freedom, Ava."

Ava's small smile at the use of her first name assured Bella she'd chosen correctly. After what they'd just admitted to each other, the required use of last names for Council-members seemed overly stiff and ridiculous. Different rules for Dragath25, just like Convict had said.

"Bella? Cadet Davies?" Winthrop's thready croak cut into their conversation. "What's going on?"

Bella sank back on her heels. Their commanding officer was alive and awake. "Don't try and get up." Ignoring protocol once again, she pressed gently down on his chest as he tried to rise. "There was a crash. You were hurt." She didn't know how much he remembered of the last day and a half. Winthrop scanned their faces, his eyes groggy, his handsome face tight with pain and weariness, his skin so pale the dark Council designation on his neck stood out even more than usual. "Are you both okay?"

"My leg's a little banged up, but I'm fine," answered Ava.

"I'm fine, too." Bella felt a surge of guilt. Beyond a few scrapes and a sore shoulder that only really hurt when something heavy bore down on it, she was remarkably unscathed while so many of their colleagues had died. She dreaded having to tell Winthrop that.

"Thank God." Winthrop's hand gripped hers. "The others?"

"Pogue and a few other soldiers also made it out alive." Her gaze slid from his. "The rest didn't."

"Shit." Lines of grief tightened his usually cheerful face. "Where is Pogue now? I—I remember somebody carrying me." He struggled to sit up fully. "I need to thank him."

She and Ava exchanged a look. "It wasn't Pogue. He and his crew deserted us."

"What?" Winthrop's protest started as a roar, but ended on a pained hiss, his hand clutching his chest. "*Christ*, that hurts." He shook off their attempt to check his bandage. "Deserted us? The Council will have Pogue's job for this. His freedom, too. His sole objective is to keep us alive."

"He was afraid for his life." Bella wasn't defending, simply explaining. She'd detested Pogue since the first time he 'accidentally' brushed up against her ass during a training session. His actions since the shuttle wreck had only confirmed her initial assumption of his character. "Our crash drew the attention of the Dragath25 prisoners."

"Are they after us?" Winthrop tried to heave himself up. Instead, he slipped on his elbow and crashed back down with a grunt.

"We're safe. Stop thrashing around." Ava added her weight to Bella's, holding the man down. Clearly, Bella wasn't the only one emboldened by being temporarily beyond Council rule. Still, her colleague's wary gaze flickered to Bella before shifting back to Winthrop. "Bella found us help."

"Help?" Winthrop's eyes slid shut. Even that simple effort had exhausted him. "Thank God. I think I need a little more time before I can make a run for it."

It was the kind of self-deprecating joke he always had at the ready. It had Bella smiling, her eyes prickling with the sting of salt, relief that he was alive, that they were all alive, winding through her.

Ava's eyes were wet, too, as she smiled down at the man. "Let me get you some water." She sprung up, hurrying toward the hollow gourd Convict had left behind.

"Bella, I'm so glad you're okay." Winthrop pressed her hand against the curve of his face, surprising her. "I knew the second I saw you, you were extraordinary. So beautiful. So determined." He turned and kissed her palm; his mouth a warm, unwelcome imprint against her skin. "I shouldn't have let Council biases deter me. I—I've wanted to tell you for so long. I...I care for you. And I'm not going to let protocol stand in my way anymore. I want us to be far more than colleagues. And my position affords enough influence to weather any damage our union might cause." His grip tightened. "Thank you for finding a way to save us so I could come to my senses."

He was in shock. Likely not thinking clearly. And, boy oh boy, the presumption. The unbelievable arrogance. Still...he was her superior. She shifted uncomfortably, her face growing hot, her mind struggling for the right thing to say.

Especially since she doubted he'd be thanking her so fervently if he knew the truth of what she'd done to save them.

"Well, isn't this cozy."

Bella looked up.

Convict loomed above, his gaze locked on Winthrop's hand atop hers. "I see he finally woke up."

Winthrop's hold tightened. "Who's this?"

The air vibrated with menace.

Bella struggled to her knees. "Convict, this is Dr. Winthrop, Senior Council Officer of our mission. Dr. Winthrop, this is Convict. The man who's saved our lives countless times already." As subtly as possible, she tried to withdraw her hand from Winthrop. He didn't let go.

Convict's nostrils flared.

Ava returned with the water, her nervous gaze flickering between the two men. "I—I wanted to thank you as well, Mr...ah, Convict. We appreciate all you've done." Ava shoved the water toward Winthrop, forcing him to free Bella's hand.

Released, Bella pushed to standing. "Did you have any trouble?"

"You worried about me, fighter girl?"

She could feel Winthrop's and Ava's gaze boring into her. It made her want to turn tail and flee. She locked her knees instead. "I'm worried about us all. I don't want anyone hurt."

Convict's gaze flickered to Winthrop before settling back on her. "Sometimes pain adds to the pleasure." He beckoned her forward, his gaze as cold and hard as when he'd faced that tigos. "This time 'round, I'll show you what I mean."

"What's he's talking about?" Winthrop's furious voice sounded behind her.

"You don't know?" A cold, half smile twisted Convict's face. "In return for all that heroism and saving your lives, I get her."

"Her?"

"Your precious Bella. To fuck. Whenever I want. However I want."

If a sinkhole would have appeared and swallowed her whole, Bella would have been grateful.

"No." Winthrop's protest was a near whisper. Ava sobbed.

Convict's attention shifted back to her. "You following me up that hill or you want to pay up in front of them?

Doesn't matter to me. I'll want you on all fours. Ass in the air."

Nausea choked her, but she swallowed past it.

She'd learned growing up that pride rarely jibed with survival. She did what she had to and moved on. Still, a part of her grieved. Despite Convict's warning, she kept fooling herself into thinking he might be something he wasn't. But it didn't matter in the end what she thought of him. He was still their best chance of getting out of here alive.

"I'll follow you." Without looking at her colleagues, she started forward.

"Bella, no," shouted Winthrop. "Ava, stop her."

Which only made Ava cry louder.

For the first time, Bella had the uncharitable wish that Winthrop had remained unconscious. She had the strong feeling none of this would be happening if he had.

"You don't need to whore yourself out to that bastard." All Winthrop's frustration at his helplessness was apparent in his voice. "We can survive without him. I'm Council, God damn it. Don't go. Don't do this to us."

Convict didn't even slow down. His utter indifference, his absolute assurance that Winthrop could do nothing to stop this, insult enough.

But Bella couldn't help herself. She turned back. "We have no weapons. No knowledge of the terrain. No food. No water. No tools. You and the rest of the our superiors said we would be safe, that this was an easy mission, a simple in and out, and you left us unprepared." Her chin tilted upward. "You don't want to thank me for what I'm doing, fine. But don't lie to me or yourself. All your Council trappings can't help us now. We won't last an hour without his help."

She didn't hurry to catch up with Convict, and he didn't slow to wait for her, either. By the time she was halfway up the rocky canyon, he'd disappeared from sight. Alone, she picked her way along the rocks, growing more and more enraged with every stumble, every scrap.

By the time she crested the top of the cliff, she was gleefully imagining using the Council rescuers' stun guns on the bastard while ordering him to crawl around on all fours. Ass in the air.

Then she crested the cliff—and sucked in a breath, her steps faltering.

CHAPTER SEVEN

Bella stared in awe, her gaze darting everywhere at once. Nestled between barren, rocky cliffs was a paradise she'd never imagined existed. A lush, green canyon dotted with towering spiky trees and fan-shaped purple and orange flora. A place even more beautiful than the one in the cave. Palms moved lazily in the wind, casting shadows over a slow moving crystal pink lake that shimmered in the suns' rays. It was…it was vibrancy and tranquility and beauty. It was sustenance. It was hope.

"Do you like it?" Convict stepped into sight from behind a large rock. The hard mask that had tightened his face when talking with Winthrop had settled into more relaxed lines.

"It's…unbelievable." Her admission was grudgingly offered. She'd liked the view better without him in it.

"I stumbled on it a few years ago. There are a couple places like it on Dragath25, but so far no one else knows about this one. I thought you'd like it."

"You meant to show it to me?"

His gaze shifted away. "I noticed how much you liked the place in the cave. I thought you might like to see this, too. The lake down there is at least fifteen degrees warmer than the one in the cave."

Like a swinging pendulum, her feelings careened back in the other direction, something almost akin to affection for Convict flaring inside.

"Amazing." She took a few awed steps closer to the cliff edge, peering down. "I can't believe it's real. I never truly believed we'd find anything useful here on Dragath25, but there it is. Plain as day. Living, thriving wild plants. Something we haven't had at home in ages." She clapped her hands in awe. "Do you know what this means? The mission wasn't a failure, after all. You may have just saved Earth."

He reared back as if slapped. "I don't give a fuck about Earth." His scowl was fierce. "What the hell has anyone there done for me except strand me on this hellhole and wait for me to die? I say Earth's demise is fitting justice."

"But millions of people will die." She slammed her fist into her hand. "You can't honestly wish them all dead. My brother and sister are there. They've done nothing to you."

He shrugged, a disturbing non-answer. "It doesn't matter what we think, anyway. We can't do a thing to change it."

"But we can." She corrected, praying she was making the right decision in confiding in him. "A search and rescue shuttle is coming. It's standard procedure after a crash. They'll come to investigate and identify survivors. They'll save us and we'll relay our findings. We'll be heroes. All of us, including you." She hurried to add the last part as his frown deepened. "Because you were the one to show me this place. I'll be very clear on that point. I'll tell the Command Council all you've done for us. I'm sure that will go a long way in reducing your sentence." She'd make sure of it. She owed him at least that.

He snorted. "For such a smart female, you really have no clue."

"Excuse me?" She drew up short.

"There's no shortening my sentence. The Command Council wants me on Dragath25 until I die and nothing will change that. And those rescuers you're counting on?" He shook his head, pity in his gaze. "They won't make it. You think your shuttle crashed by accident?"

An inky cloud of dread spread through her veins. "What are you saying?"

"I'm saying the Council has no idea what's going on here. I'm saying you're hardly the first research vessel to try and land here. I'm saying 225's pack brought down your shuttle, just like the few that came before, and they'll do the same to whomever comes next."

"That's not true."

He started toward her. "Is that why you've been so accommodating? Were you holding out hope for rescue? Imagining that this little deal of ours only needed to be for the short term? That you'd only have to suffer some Dragath25 lowlife's cock inside you for a few days more?" His laugh had no humor in it. "Sorry, fighter girl, but there's no imminent rescue in sight."

"You're lying. They're coming."

"225's pack only lets the droids through because they like what they bring—food, clothes, and bodies for slave labor or fucking—and they haven't wanted Command Council to get suspicious until they were ready to take them on."

"Take them on?"

"You think you can leave a group of criminals alone for thousands of years and not have them build their own societies? All it takes is one visionary psychopath with the ability to terrorize enough followers into doing whatever he wants and you go from a disorganized penal planet full of kill-or-be-killed criminals to a well-organized terrorist training center. And that is what Dragath25 has become."

"That can't be."

"You may not have heard on Earth because of the Council's censorship, but this planet is now run by a vicious pack of killers with delusions of grandeur and a fairly large grudge against the Council. To top it off, they've figured out how to jam entering ship's electronic systems, causing them to crash without much warning at all. From what I've seen, they're on their way to building the kind of machinery that can do far more. Maybe even get them off this planet and into space." He hoisted the backpack that was never far from his side. "All they're missing is a few critical pieces and some know-how. But those will eventually come."

"No." She took a step back. Then another. "You're lying. Rescue is coming. And I'm going to get off here. Ava and Dr. Winthrop, too."

"Careful," Convict barked, his backpack hitting the dirt as he raised his hands and beckoned her toward him. "You're near the edge."

She barely heard him. "We're going to tell them about the plants. How they're able to thrive in harsh heat and dirt similar to Earth's changing environment. They're going to agree on the need for further study, and we're going to give Earth and my sister and my brother a fighting chance at living a full life."

"Stop." He sounded furious. And cruel.

She shook her head, tears blurring her face. "I'm not listening to you anymore." Her boot slipped near the edge, but she kept stepping backwards, needing distance, needing a barrier from the awful things he was telling her. "Stay back."

The ground gave way beneath her feet.

She screamed. Just as strong hands seized her forearms.

"*God damn it.*" Convict hauled her close, pulling her back from the edge as the sound of falling rocks echoed in her ears. "What did I tell you that first day, female?" He shook her gently. "You need to give up your dreams of Earth. You need to come to grips with the fact that you're on Dragath25 now." He jerked her close again. "You *have* to do that or you'll never survive."

"I thought you meant for the short term," she shouted back, pushing at his chest. "I didn't think you meant forever. Tell me you're lying."

"I can't."

"No!" She struggled to get away. From his words. From the sincerity in his gaze. From the awful truth of what this meant for her brother and sister.

If she was declared missing or dead, Council contracts stated that all dependents would be removed from protective Council housing and resource distribution. Her sweet, young sister and brother would be sent back to the orphan barracks where she'd grown up. A soulless, miserable place where starvation, death, and predators were a way of life. And this time she wouldn't be there to protect them.

"You're wrong," she insisted. "A rescue shuttle is coming to save us." She pressed. Shoved. And all the time he held her. His grip firm, but not painful. Just waiting it out. Waiting her out.

Until her pants gave way to sobs and her arms fell lifelessly at her side. "I don't…I don't want to be here forever."

Expression grim, he pulled her close, holding her tight. His big, strong hands running up and down her spine, her only anchor. "It's okay, fighter girl. It's okay."

But it wasn't. She wasn't sure it would ever be again.

Convict held her tight trying to comfort them both. Even on Earth, he hadn't been so good at it. He'd been a pilot and a soldier, and even when home on leave from Command Council business, he and his wife had led fairly separate lives. He'd understood. He was home so infrequently. She had to make a life for herself. But he hadn't understood when she'd started sleeping with the married Council representative of their district.

"Convict?"

"Yeah?" He didn't mean to sound so gruff, but she was staring up at him, her gorgeous face streaked with tears, her fingers curled against his chest, and his throat had gone a little tight.

He'd thought for an instant he'd lost her over the cliff, that he wouldn't be fast enough to reach her in time, and his heart was still coming to grips with the matter. Which was dumber than dumb. Growing attached to anything on Dragath25 was a recipe for disappointment.

"No one's coming?" Her voice sounded small. Not like his fighter girl at all.

Still, he wouldn't give her anything but the truth. "They're coming, but they won't make it out alive."

She shuddered against him. "I can't just let it happen."

He played with the ends of her hair, reveling in the soft brush of silk against his palms. "There's no way to stop it. Surviving on this planet is hard enough. Trying to take on 225 and his pack will only get you killed alongside them."

"But to do nothing…." Her words ended on a sob.

"Remember what I told you." He tried to keep the edge from his voice, but it wasn't easy. Her softness—any softness—reminded him of his initial conclusion that she wouldn't last long—and that already displeased him more than it should. "Earth rules don't apply here. Worry for yourself."

She didn't respond. He didn't say anything more, either. Just savored the pleasure of holding her warm and willing and trusting against him.

"Convict?" He should have known the silence wouldn't last. His fighter girl was a talker. "Why'd you say those things before? Why'd you make Winthrop and Ava think you were taking me up here to fuck me?"

His dick twitched. He liked hearing that word from her full lips. "Because that's what I intend to do."

She studied him, as if she could see to the heart of him. Which was impossible. He'd lost that particular organ a long time ago. "And the part about the pain?"

He shifted uncomfortably. "That might have been a slight exaggeration." He tipped her chin to meet his hard stare. "But you're mine now. Not his. And there's not a fucking thing that Council-asshole can do about it laid out there on the ground so he better get used to it. You both better get used to it."

"I don't want to be with him. I didn't, even before the crash." She didn't even hesitate.

Something inside him loosened. Something he hadn't even realized had been squeezing his chest tight. "Good."

"I know I have no real ground to ask given the terms of our deal," her voice cracked, lashing at him like a whip, "but I–I would appreciate it if you didn't purposely humiliate me."

Shit. When he'd seen her hand clasped with that smug, blueblood scientist's, he'd wanted to blot it out anyway he could. To make it clear as day that she wasn't the bastard's to touch anymore. And, maybe yes, to make her feel like shit—as low and dirty and shitty as he felt knowing he'd never measure up to a well-respected, well-paid Council scientist with a bunch of fancy degrees and no criminal record.

Which made him a grade-A asshole. And stupid, too.

Because the truth of the matter was, he didn't want his fighter girl to feel badly about being with him. He didn't want her to hate it. Or be desperate to get on that shuttle and travel light years away.

Because the fact was, he liked her.

He liked the way she smelled. The way she tasted. Like vanilla and woman and light and hope and goodness and all the things he hadn't had in forever. He liked the curve of her waist and the fullness of her breasts. He liked the little sounds she made when he drove inside her. He liked her spirit. Her courage and the way she looked out for her colleagues and her siblings. He liked her toughness and her tenacity. Her resilience and her sense of fairness. Even her fierceness when he was being an ass.

Hell, she was damn near perfect. The kind of woman he'd never thought to find. Not only on Dragath25, but anywhere in the universe.

"I won't do that again." He tilted her chin so she could see the sincerity in his gaze.

She smiled. "And I shouldn't have lashed out at you for telling me the truth about the rescue shuttle or the way things stand. I won't do that again, either."

"We'll call it even."

It was weird conversing like this. Holding her like this. Like a normal person.

Weird. And nice. And terrifying. Because he wasn't a normal person anymore, and Dragath25 wasn't a normal place.

"Even." She repeated his wording. "I like that." She looked pleased. Just as he knew she would. Then a shadow crossed her face. "Are we safe from this 225 and his pack?"

"No one's safe on this planet, but I know how 225 and his pack operate and where they like to spend their time. As long as I don't bother them, they don't bother me. They know I could make more trouble for them than they want."

"So they won't come for us?"

He'd been asking himself the same question. "They know there were survivors at the crash. I did my best to hide your tracks, but those soldiers of yours weren't so careful. Hopefully, your soldiers will keep 225's pack busy enough and they'll never realize there were additional survivors."

If the pack discovered some of those still alive from the crash were women, there wouldn't be anything that would keep them away. Which was why he'd been pushing so hard to get as far from the crash site as fast as he could.

"What if Pogue and the others tell?" she asked.

He doubted they'd even be given a chance to scream for mercy. 225 and his pack were more feral than tigos. But he also knew that, despite the way those soldier bastards had deserted her, she wouldn't like to hear his answer. So he went with a distraction. "You trying to renege on our deal?"

"What? No." She looked adorably confused, and a little angry. He preferred it to the scared look of a moment before.

He swiveled her around before she could protest, drawing her up against the full length of his body, letting her feel the hard press of his thickening dick against her ass. "You sure about that?" His mouth skimmed the length of her neck. God, he loved the way she smelled. "Because I might have been exaggerating about the pain, but not the rest. It's payment time and I want you on all fours. Now."

CHAPTER EIGHT

At Convict's urging, Bella sank to her knees. He followed right behind, his hard body brooking no argument.

Confusion swirled within. On edge, uncertain, her mind whirled. Dragath25 might be her future forever. She might never see her sister and brother again.

But she didn't want to think of that. Or of her colleagues who'd died on that shuttle. Or of the fate of the search and rescue team she couldn't help. For just a few minutes she didn't want to think of anything but how good it felt to be in Convict's powerful arms. How the sound of his voice, low and husky and commanding, made her skin hot and her pussy wet.

A low moan slipped from her as his callused hands slid beneath her shirt to play with her breasts, tugging her nipples, making her shiver. Her body arched into his touch.

Then his palm was against her back, pressing her forward until she was on all fours, her elbows in the dirt, her ass lifted. Just as he'd said she would be.

Air shivered across her lower body as he slid her pants down and off. And for a second, she was alone, waiting, and then his hands glided up her thighs to cover her ass, raising gooseflesh.

Truth be told, she liked this position. Liked the vulnerability. The fact that she didn't know what part of her he'd touch next. Still, she started when a warm soft tongue licked the length of her, making her shudder, her body tingled with pleasure.

"Oh, God." Every nerve sprung alive. "That feels so good."

He gave a low chuckle against her pussy, eating her out, devouring her as if she was the sweetest cream. And with every lick, with every rasp of his tongue against her swollen bundle of nerves, he wound her tighter and tighter. Her legs spreading wide as she bucked against him. Desperate to come and wanting to ride the ecstasy forever.

Then he slid two fingers inside her, and there was no choice. She splintered apart, wave after wave of pleasure crashing through her as she came and came and came.

She was still coming, her breath a frantic pant, as he grabbed her hips and held her in place, working his cock deep into her slick pussy, inch by inch, until his balls were pressed against her ass and he loomed above her.

"You like that?'

"Yes."

His fingers found her clit, claiming, playing. "Things don't seem so bad right now, do they, fighter girl?" His hand stilled. "Do they?"

He actually wanted an answer?

"No," she gasped, rocking back against him. The stroke of his hand making her desperate for a second release. For more oblivion. "They're good. Very, very good."

"Exactly." His finger skimmed over her clit and upward through her folds to finger her tight rosebud. "We can do whatever we want here. However we want." His finger pressed at the tight hole, demanding entrance.

She let out an involuntary moan. The foreign touch making her burn. The discomfort of being stretched leaving her no choice but to be in the present, to surrender to the here and now of his touch.

"Pain and pleasure." His voice was a dark rasp against her ear. "That's how you know you're alive, fighter girl. That's how you know you've got something left to give."

It was as if he saw to the heart of her struggle.

Her breath devolved to shallow pants as he worked in deeper until she could feel his knuckle against her ass. White hot pleasure rocketed through her as his other hand worked her clit, his fingers driving in and out in tandem with his cock, filling her, taking her over, making her feel alive, more in touch with herself—with the moment—than she'd ever been.

"Come with me," he demanded—and she did. Beyond all burdens. Beyond pain or worry to sheer, white-hot bliss. Her fingers clawing at the dirt as the shattering orgasm ripped through her. Their slick bodies cleaving together as wave after wave of pleasure hurtled them both over the edge.

Spent, her knees gave out, and she would have buckled to the ground if not for Convict. Catching her, he pulled her up so that she rested against his chest, a sated rag doll, her breathing still coming hard and fast, her body alive with blissful aftershocks. All the while, he thrust slowly inside her, his movement almost gentle now.

She turned and smiled back at him.

And was amazed to see his eyes crinkle and his lips turn upward as he returned the grin. That look of wonder back in his gaze.

Comprehension crashed over her. Sure, they'd fucked like animals, but there'd still been something redemptive, something hopeful in their joining. Brutal. Fierce. But honest. Exciting. Real.

Ava and Winthrop might not understand, but she didn't care. It wasn't even about the deal anymore. It was about her and Convict. About the way he made her feel.

She wasn't giving up on getting off this planet and back to her family, but she was beginning to realize there were lessons to be learned in the meantime.

All her life, all she'd done was try to endure. But, here, where she'd least expected, she'd glimpsed another way. Maybe her stay on Dragath25 didn't have to be as bleak as she'd imagined. Maybe it didn't have to be only about survival. Maybe there was room for joy and pleasure, too.

"Convict?" She waited until his gaze found hers. "I'm glad it was you who got to that crash site first."

He sucked in a breath.

She was still waiting for a response when a shrill whistle rent the air.

"Wait." Convict's arm around her belly stopped her in her tracks.

She'd fumbled into her pants and immediately started running back toward camp at the sound of the alarm.

"Ava and Winthrop are in danger." She strained against his hold. "I have to help."

"Just slow down." He pulled her against him as if she weighed nothing. "We need to see what's down there."

"But if it's a tigos…."

"They're already dead." He pushed her up against a rock. "Stay here. I'll come for you as soon as it's safe."

"No way. I can help. I—"

"No argument."

She ground her teeth in frustration. "Fine. But if you take too long, if I think you're in trouble, I'm coming."

He shot her an annoyed look, but he didn't stay to debate. Instead, he wedged his pack in a small crevice above her head, smeared dirt from a nearby rock on his face and chest, and took off at a run.

She held her breath, listening for any sound, but everything was silent, no clues offered as to what he and the others faced below. She kicked the dirt, counted back from one hundred, and was already deciding she'd wait only one minute more when….

He appeared, his expression ominous. "It's that soldier bastard and some of his men."

Relief sent her staggering back against the rock. "That's not so bad then."

Now wasn't the time to hold a grudge. Pogue and his fellow soldiers had guns. And combat knowledge. With them around, chances for survival had just increased. Plus, they might not be entirely reliable, but they were familiar. She could use a little bit of that right now.

"I don't know," said Convict. "None of them look too happy."

It was her turn to frown. "There was little love lost between the scientists and the soldiers even before the crash. I bet Winthrop ripped Pogue a new one for leaving us." She chewed on her lip, thinking. "What do you think?"

"I think I'd rather ignore the summons." He covered her mouth when she started to protest. "But I know you're only going to badger me until we see what's up. So we'll go down. But you stay behind me the whole time. If I tell you to run, you do exactly that. No argument. No hesitation. Understood?"

She nodded. He hadn't taken his hand away so there was really no choice.

Plus, that same dread that had roiled around in her gut right before the shuttle crash was back. Still, she had to go. These were her colleagues. They needed to be warned about 225 and the jamming device.

"Let's go."

Pogue and his fellow soldiers sighted them before they were halfway down the ridge, their guns training on Convict without hesitation. It was tempting to step out from behind him and shout that neither she nor Convict was a threat, but she didn't. For all she knew, she might have the opposite effect of stirring things up.

The second Convict's boot touched flat ground, the tension in the air ramped up another hundred degrees. Interestingly, there were only seven other soldiers with Pogue now, down from the ten who'd survived the crash. Were they creeping up from behind to surround them? Or off somewhere else? She didn't even want to contemplate the third alternative.

"Cadet West, come out nice and slow." Officer Pogue, his chest puffed with smug self-importance, pointed his gun straight at Convict's head. Convict's spear lay broken in half at Pogue's feet. "This scumbag can't hurt you anymore."

Winthrop had obviously been talking—and not in a way that would earn Convict any sympathy.

"I'm fine," she assured.

"The soldiers are here to protect us, Bella. You're safe now." Winthrop peered out from behind Pogue, the whistle alarm Convict had given her gripped tightly in his hand. "And this one is about to learn what happens to those who ignore Council protocol."

Apparently, Winthrop had decided to overlook both Pogue's desertion and her defiant parting shot, but not Convict's disrespect.

"I really am fine." She stayed where she was. It didn't escape her notice that she might be the only thing preventing Pogue and the others from opening fire. "This man"—she preferred not to call him Convict just then for obvious reasons—"wasn't hurting me. He's *never* hurt me. He's one of the good guys."

Was it her imagination or did Convict nearly stumble?

"You don't need to pretend or feed his ego anymore," insisted Pogue. "We're here now."

"He saved us from a dust storm and a vicious beast. He kept us sheltered from the other prisoners on the planet. He gave us water and food and kept us alive. You need to lower your weapons."

Their weapons stayed up.

It probably didn't help that Convict, with that dirt for camouflage, looked more like a wild creature than a man.

"This is bullshit. The guy's no savior. Come out from behind him." Pogue's scowl was deeper than before. "Then we'll lower our weapons."

She got the distinct sense Pogue didn't like her refusal to let him play hero.

"I'm telling you the truth. This man is on our side. But there are a group of prisoners who run this planet who aren't. They're the ones who brought down our ship." She ignored the skeptical stares of Pogue and his men. "They're planning to do the same to the rescue shuttle coming for us. We have to find a way to stop them."

"Your captor's been telling you lies." Pogue's grip on his gun tightened. "Don't let him manipulate you into trusting him."

"Bella, come over here," coaxed Winthrop, "and we'll gladly talk about your concerns."

"Convict?" she prodded at a whisper. "Any good ideas?"

"Just stay where you are." His voice was low, his breathing steady. "It won't be long now."

Won't be long now? He made no sense.

Realizing it was up to her, she shifted tactics. "Cadet Davies, Dr. Winthrop, you know he saved both your lives. Tell them."

Winthrop's mouth flat lined. She'd get no help there.

Ava looked far more torn. "Did he hurt you? He said...he said there'd be pain."

Damn Convict and his stupid anger.

"No, he didn't hurt me, Ava." She deliberately used her colleague's first name. "I swear it. This time was no different than the other times. He made me feel good."

Convict's low chuckle surprised—and irritated—her. Of all the times to find something to laugh about. She pinched his waist, or tried to. He was so hard there was very little to hold onto.

"I'm trying to fix things," she whispered in exasperation.

"Which I appreciate. But bragging about my prowess is only pissing Winthrop and Pogue off more."

She dared a quick peek. Convict was right. Both men looked downright murderous.

"You send her out right now," shouted Winthrop, "or they're going to shift their guns from stun to kill."

"He saved your life," she yelled right back.

"I'm curious about something." Convict's calm words were more arresting than any shout. "How'd you find us? I thought I covered our tracks fairly well."

The crazy man acted as if he hadn't even heard Winthrop's threat.

Pogue looked annoyed. "We didn't need to follow any tracks. Dr. Winthrop has a tracking device imbedded in his skin for the rescue team to lock on. It keeps working as long as he's alive. All we needed to do was follow that and here you are."

No wonder Pogue had returned. He hadn't had a change of heart or been concerned about their wellbeing. He'd realized Winthrop had survived and come back to be near the Doctor so he'd be rescued, too.

"Is that standard procedure?" Convict sounded only remotely curious.

She and Ava exchanged a look. They both knew it wasn't. Usually, the tracking device was on the ship. Emergency training drills stressed the need for survivors to stay near the ship specifically so the rescue team could find them near the crash-site. Of course, Winthrop's family was very high up among the Council elite so perhaps that had triggered the change in policy.

"What does it matter?" Winthrop looked almost uncomfortable. "I have one. They found us. And you're not in charge, *Convict*. I am. Council protocol remains in effect even on this hellhole." His lip curled upward. "Bella, come out now or you could both get hurt."

Indecision whispered through her. She didn't want Convict hurt. "Maybe I should go?"

"Stay right where you are," he demanded.

The quiet click of Pogue's gun cocking echoed like a shout. "We're done waiting." We? Wasn't it Winthrop's decision to make? Suddenly, a lot more than Convict's fate seemed to be unraveling.

Acting on impulse, she pushed Convict aside—or tried to. The man refused to budge, grabbing her elbow and hauling her back behind him. At the same time, a figure stepped in front of Pogue's gun.

"Ava, no. Get back." Bella's voice was shrill and tight.

"No." Ava stood unsteadily on her one good leg, her gaze locked on Pogue. "You don't get to decide what happens next." Her gaze shifted to Winthrop. "Nor, forgive me for saying this, should you, no matter what Council protocol dictates. Dragath25 is not Earth. She might not be a Council-descendant, but Bella has earned the right to be heard, her judgments respected." For once, a haughty, Council tone infused Ava's voice. "She's done more to keep us alive than anyone else. She's the real hero here."

Touched and awed, and a lot embarrassed, by her colleague's words, Bella sent her a shaky smile. Somehow, some way, Ava had become a friend—and found her strength.

But one side-glance at the malice in Pogue's gaze as he stared at Ava and Bella's smile faded. It was clear Ava had also gained an enemy for life.

Before Bella could try to lessen the tension, a dark, long shadow skimmed over the ground, blotting out the sun.

"Holy shit." Three of Pogue's soldiers swung their guns to point at the sky.

She looked up, her breath leaving in a rush. Like something out of the prehistoric Earth stories of old, a giant, orange bird-like creature with wings nearly the width of their shuttle soared above, its hooked, sharp beak opening as it let out a shrill shriek. One that sounded strangely familiar.

"Oh, *God*." She stood frozen in horror as it dove closer and closer.

All around her chaos erupted as everyone started yelling, some calling to run, some to shoot. All except for Convict.

Calm as ever, he pulled her from behind him, his arm going around her waist as he walked them both slowly backward the way they'd come. "It's a saybak. It came when it heard the mating call from Winthrop's whistle." His tone was shockingly nonchalant. Like he had all day to explain. Like they were not about to be eaten by a living, breathing dinosaur. "I designed it purposely to give me an added advantage. Saybak's can't resist the sound and they have great hearing."

"Uh-huh." She nodded, barely listening, her gaze locked in terror on the approaching creature.

"Though they look menacing, they're actually harmless—"

"Fire," shouted Pogue.

A stream of red lasers sliced the air.

"—Until you do that," finished Convict.

The creature shrieked in fury, its orange feathers shifting to bright red. With a hiss, it unleashed a line of flames from its mouth. One soldier screamed, managing by inches to dodge the line of fire.

"Go! Go, now." Convict pushed her back up the cliff. "They're distracted."

"But they're going to be killed. We can't leave them."

In the next instant, she was upside down, slung over his shoulder.

"I knew you were going to be a pain in the ass about this," he mumbled, breaking into a run.

"Let me go." She wouldn't hurt him, but she could try and twist herself off. Squirming wildly, she leveraged herself up, her eyes locking with Ava's as her colleague found cover under a rocky ledge.

A sharp sting landed across her ass, freezing her in place.

"Stop fighting and listen. Saybaks can't keep attacking like that. It takes time to recharge. It will turn and flee in less than twenty seconds. Your colleagues are going to be okay."

She took a second to absorb his words, jostling upside down all the while. "Ava?"

"With us gone, there'll be less reason for your friend to risk herself for you."

Bella let out a long sigh. "Then put me down and let's get the hell out of here." Better to wait and talk to Pogue and Winthrop without Convict or Ava around. In the meantime, Winthrop would watch out for Ava. And Pogue would keep Winthrop alive since the Council-connected Doctor was his ticket home.

Bella's world went topsy-turvy once again as Convict set her on her feet. He dragged her along, his arm around her for balance, until she found her equilibrium. Then she was charging up the cliff on her own steam, his big body right behind her, pushing her on. He didn't even let her catch her breath when they reached the top. Merely snagged his pack from the hidey-hole and corralled her down a different path. Since he was leading them toward the Oasis, she didn't complain. Plus, she could barely breathe. Much less talk.

It wasn't until a lot later when everything was silent and they were once again on flat ground that she found enough breath to actually speak. "Where are we going?"

"Home."

Her steps faltered. She hadn't really thought in terms of Convict and a home. It had an odd sense of permanency. One she definitely wasn't ready for. She'd been thinking more in terms of a few hours or, at most, a day away from her crew. "Is...is it far from here?"

"Far enough." His hand was firm against her lower back as he propelled her onward, farther and farther from everything and everyone she'd ever known. "They won't bother us. No one will."

She wasn't sure whether to be comforted or terrified by his assertion.

CHAPTER NINE

"Is it much farther?" Bella scanned the horizon, trying to remember if they'd turned left or right at the last split in the rocky cliffs. Covered in miles of the same rust rock and debris, it was hard to tell one part of the terrain from another. The Oasis had definitely looked a lot closer from the top of the cliff.

Which was making it especially hard for her to feel confident about her ability to return to her colleagues' campsite on her own if necessary.

"A little ways more." One hand around his spear, one hand at her lower back, Convict urged her forward, his gaze scanning everywhere, his shoulders tense.

It was the same response he'd given her a half hour ago.

"Can you tell me more about this jammer? Where they keep it? How hard it was to make?"

"Why?" His voice had gone hard.

"I'm curious."

"I told you before, there's no going up against 225 and his pack. They number at least three thousand and fifty men, each more psychotic than the last. And they show no mercy. If they get hold of you, you'll long for death."

A shudder passed through her. "Still, there has to be some way to stop them."

"Not without dying yourself."

They walked in silence for a long while.

"I'm sorry about my colleagues." She couldn't stand the quiet any more. It was giving her too much time to think, especially about whether she'd made the right choice to leave with Convict. "They're frightened and unsure and lashing out at everything as a threat. I'll be able to get through to them next time we talk."

If he noticed her subtle reference to seeing them again, he didn't remark on it.

"They're smart to be on guard," he said instead. "It's the only way to stay alive on this planet. Still it won't make a bit of difference. Most of them will be dead within the month."

At her soft gasp, his scowl deepened.

"You need to toughen up." His hold tightened on his spear. "Don't forget those soldiers are the same bastards who left you and your friends to die that first day. They deserve everything that's coming to them."

Disturbed, Bella said nothing. But inside, doubts battered at her. She kept trusting the humanity she'd glimpsed inside Convict, kept telling herself the way he touched her was more significant than what he said, but could she be fooling herself? Had she truly chosen the wrong side with which to stand? Ava's reminder that there was a reason that Convict was a prisoner on Dragath25 echoed ominously through her head. Worse, hadn't he himself warned her he wasn't one of the good guys?

Questions clogged her throat, too many to let out at once. If his claims about what would happen to anyone who tried to rescue them were true, what did that mean for their deal? Was he thinking to use her for a while and then bring her back to the others when he got tired of her? Should she turn back now? Return to the soldiers and Winthrop and take her chances?

Maybe she should slip away when he relaxed his guard....It might be easier for both of them in the end.

She snuck a sideways glance at his profile. Convict's shoulders were taut, deep lines bracketing his eyes as he shifted his gaze between her and their surroundings. He definitely didn't look like a man who'd be relaxing his guard any time soon. And still the hand on her back propelled her on.

It was at least another half an hour before she tried talking again.

"How did you find this home of yours?" Goodness knows it wasn't easily accessible.

"By accident."

She waited. Nothing more. "Are you deliberately shutting me out or do you just not realize I'm trying to make conversation?"

He didn't stop walking, but his brow crinkled. "Maybe a little of both."

"Well, at least you're honest." Though a lifetime on Dragath25 with someone who refused to share any part of himself would be a long sentence, indeed.

"I always tell the truth."

He looked so serious she nodded solemnly. "Good to know."

He hopped over a large rock and then turned to help her. He'd been doing that a lot. Probably best to concentrate on nice things like that rather than her worries.

Then he surprised her by volunteering information she hadn't even asked. "This side of the planet is a lot more isolated. Most convicts keep to the other side where the Council built barracks. That side is also where the Council does the droid drops; and because it's so bleak, it's also less popular with tigos and other predatory animals."

"I can see the appeal," she joked.

"No, you can't." He didn't smile. "The penal barracks are...bad." Ugly memories tightened his jaw, making her wish she hadn't been so cavalier. "It's a free-for-all over there, but the days the droids drop off the fresh meat are the worst."

"Fresh meat?"

"That's what they call the new prisoners."

She shuddered, remembering the wild shrieks.

Convict looked equally haunted. "Only the strong survive."

Suddenly, his conviction that you can't save them all made a lot more sense. He'd had to watch the new arrivals being raped and beaten and torn apart. No wonder he'd turned so hard.

According to the required lessons taught to all non-Council youths, Earth had been just as lawless and violent until the Command Council established order. Clearly though, the Council remained unconcerned about what happened beyond the planetary boundaries.

Unable to resist any longer, she reached out, resting her hand on Convict's forearm. Pale skin against bronzed flesh. The heat of his skin warming her own. "So you left?"

His gaze locked on her hand. "I wasn't interested in becoming a 225 pack member. But this side of the planet has its costs, too. There are more frequent dust storms and it's tigos territory, which is why most prisoners won't come here—or if they do, they don't last." His hand covered hers, almost as if he couldn't help himself. "I was running from a tigos female and her three babies when I stumbled across the Oasis. I barely made it out of that skirmish alive."

Her chest squeezed. "I'm glad you did." Slowly, but surely, he was sharing about himself, about his life—and everything he told her made her only admire him more.

She couldn't imagine believing as he did that he would live and die on Dragath25 without any hope of rescue or pardon. It had to twist a person. And yet, Convict hadn't let the violence and ugliness of this place destroy him. He might be hard, but he'd never been cruel or brutal.

Her chest fluttered. He really was an extraordinary man.

Oh no. Her heart beat fast at the direction of her thoughts. She was coming to care for him. More than she should. In a way that went beyond gratitude. Beyond lust.

A bead of sweat rolled down her spine. That wouldn't do. Not when he could never leave Dragath25 and she had to go. Not when she couldn't afford to grow attached.

She sucked down a deep breath and opened her mouth to tell him she was going back.

"Hold up." Convict's grip halted her in place, her deep breath—and her declaration—still caught in her lungs. He cocked his head, listening.

She mirrored his actions, her heart thumping away.

Had he heard a tigos? Or another sayback? She didn't love learning this was the primary territory of the tigos. If she had her way, she'd never see another one again in her whole life.

But as hard as she tried to hear something, nothing but the bleak, desolate silence of the cliffs and the occasional whistling wind reached her eardrums.

"I don't hear anything," she whispered.

He said nothing, his frown lengthening.

They stood frozen so long her legs grew stiff. Then, suddenly, he startled her with a low, fierce whisper. "See that large boulder straight ahead? About the height of two men?" At her nod, he pressed his spear into her hand. Next, he gave her his pack. "Go there, crouch down with your back against the rock so you can see what's coming—and don't move."

"Where are you going?"

"I heard something."

Her hands clutched his bicep. "So let's investigate together." She definitely didn't want to be left behind.

He shook his head. Peeled her hand from him. "Go, now." His words were an unquestionable order. "Do not move until I come for you."

Had Convict been a soldier? His tone screamed military. So did the way he disappeared in the blink of an eye. And why was she thinking about this now as she hurried to do his bidding, her back pressing against the hard rock as she crouched on shaky legs, the spear gripped tight in both hands, the pack between her feet? Probably because she was terrified and a million random thoughts were running through her mind.

Pull it together, Bella.

Sucking down a deep breath and then another, she forced herself to calm down. To remember all she had already overcome. A minute later, her breathing was far steadier. Enough for her to hear absolute silence. No sound of footsteps. Or a scuffle. Not even a shout.

She waited several more minutes. Flexed her legs. Scanned the limited perimeter. Still no Convict.

After what felt like hours, she popped up, stretching her legs as she used her higher perspective to see a little bit more of the area. Still no luck sighting him.

She took a tentative step away from the rock. Then another. Yes, he'd told her to stay, but he could be in trouble. Cowering and leaving others to solve the problem had never been her way. Plus, she was the one with the spear. That had to count for something.

Moving in the direction he'd been facing when he disappeared, she hopped over rocks and crevices, the heavy weight of the spear making her slower than she would have liked.

Suddenly, a thump sounded. Like something had leapt from the cliff behind—a cliff she'd failed to scan thoroughly.

"Fuck, yeah." It was a rough, soulless voice she didn't recognize. "Live pussy."

Her spear hand came up, but it was already too late.

A meaty forearm closed around her throat, yanking her backwards until her legs dangled off the ground. Her spear slipped from her grasp.

The scent of rotted fish burned her nostrils.

"And 225 thought there were only male soldiers on board." Indifferent to the clawing against his arm, her oversized captor pressed his nose into her hair, black spots clouding her vision as her lungs grew more and more desperate for air. "Must be my lucky fucking night."

She was slammed onto her stomach atop a flat boulder, her lungs dragging in a frantic breath as pain reverberated through her ribs and hipbones.

A hand gripped the nape of her neck and held her down. "I'm supposed to bring back what I find." He chuckled. "But this will be our little secret, right?"

In shock, it took her a moment to register that her legs were dangling over the rock.

Her attacker was already yanking her pants over her ass when she kicked back, her boot heels connecting with his thigh. Unfortunately, all her blow did was piss him off.

The hand against her neck dug in, choking off her air, no matter how she fought. "Feel free to struggle. They all do." Hairy thighs flattened her legs harder against the rough rock scraping away skin. "You'll end up raped and dead all the same."

A curious sense of detachment rolled over her. A comforting hum sounding in her ear as her air gave out. The pain lifting away. She'd come so far. But even she wasn't going to survive this.

Suddenly, the horrible weight of her attacker disappeared. Followed by the loud thwack of flesh against flesh. In a daze, she sucked in a desperate breath and swiveled round.

Convict.

Chest heaving, face harder than she'd ever seen, he grappled with a bald giant two heads taller with narrow grey eyes and a flat, blunt nose. Her stomach jumped to her throat.

They crashed into one of the boulders and then another. Fists flying. Grunts and curses exploding from both men. Her scream of warning strangling in her throat as Convict ducked a vicious swing before popping up to deliver a lightning-fast blow to the giant's jaw. Then she blinked, and her attacker fell backwards against a sharp rock,

Convict's fists plowing into the man's face and gut in rapid fire. His strength, his quickness, astonishing.

But Convict's opponent was no weakling either. With a roar, he launched himself forward, his arms swingy wildly.

She pushed off the rock, her movements clumsy as she jerked up her pants. She needed to find her spear. She needed to help.

But even as her plan formed, slow and sluggish in her mind, Convict sidestepped the man easily, using his momentum to ensure the attacker stumbled past. Then, as quick as a tigos, Convict's powerful arms locked round the man's neck.

Her gaze fused with Convict's.

They were as black and unreadable as ever.

His arms twisted. There was a faint crack. Her attacker's body twitched.

Her mouth opened on a silent scream.

Convict dropped his arms.

Her attacker crumpled to the ground, his narrow grey eyes open and empty.

Convict had killed for her.

CHAPTER TEN

Bella stared at the dead man.

"You okay?" Convict stepped over the body, his chest heaving. "Did he hurt you?"

At the reminder, she clutched her sore throat, her gaze shifting between him and the dead guy.

Convict stepped in front, blocking her view, corralling her backwards down the path away from the dead man. "Don't waste a minute on 015. He tortured and killed eleven women before being sent to Dragath25. Someone should have killed him long ago."

Another shudder swept through her.

"Bella?" He raised his hands. She blinked stupidly. He'd used her name. Her real name. She wasn't even sure he knew it.

"Yes?" Did he mean to hold her? God she hoped so; she could really use his strength right now. But in the next moment, his hands dropped back to his sides, curling into fists.

"You sure you're okay?"

The gentleness in his voice had her blinking back tears. Or maybe it was the disappointment that she was still standing on her own.

"I'm okay." Her words were a whispered croak. Worse, the strange lassitude that had seized hold of her moments ago was drifting away to leave behind a pounding headache, twisting stomach, and shaking legs. Still, it could have been far worse. "You got there in time. You saved me."

She wrapped her arms around herself, her trembling growing stronger with every second. "How about you? Are you okay?"

He looked down at his hands as if thinking about it for the first time. Blood and scratches covered his knuckles. "I'm fine." His gaze found hers. There was challenge in his stare. "He deserved what he got."

"And I couldn't be more grateful you were there to dispense justice." If he thought she was going to be berate him for killing a monster intent on torturing and killing her, he was wrong.

He nodded absently. Plowed a hand through his hair. Even from an arm's length away, she could feel his keyed up energy, the darkness still roiling through him.

"Where did he come from?" It seemed the logical thing to ask, and yet the words felt strange coming out of her mouth. Like she should be screaming instead. Or falling apart.

"He was a tracker for 225. He and a few others must have been following your soldiers' tracks from the crash site."

A fresh surge of panic whipped through her. "A few others?"

"They won't be bothering you."

It took her a second to understand. Convict had killed them, too.

He could have easily walked away, but he hadn't. Instead, he'd gone on the hunt and taken them out before they could hurt anyone else.

Another wave of gratitude—and something more primitive—flowed through her. He'd warned her there was no humanity and no selflessness on Dragath25, but he'd lied. "Thank you."

His expression turned wary. "Don't think this is the end. 225 will send more men to investigate. Especially when these don't return. He doesn't like any challenge to his authority."

"We've got to warn the others."

"Not tonight."

"But—"

"Not tonight. It will take at least a couple of days for 225 and his pack to sense something is wrong. That gives us plenty of time to cover our tracks and come up with a plan to convince them any survivors are now dead."

She almost wept; she was so relieved. The thought of retracing their steps and handling another ugly confrontation with Pogue and Dr. Winthrop was more than she could handle right then. And Convict's plan was a good one. "Do…do we need to bury the bodies?"

He shook his head. "Dragath25 will take care of that. By morning, there'll be no evidence left to find."

Another shudder ran through her. Convict was right. This planet really was a hellhole. She couldn't believe he'd survived so long.

Finally, they reached the spot where he'd told her to wait. His pack was still there.

"Stop a minute," he said. "I want to check your injuries."

"I'm fine."

A muscle twitched in his jaw. "Do it anyway."

On a low sigh, she stood still, tilting her head up so he could see her neck. She wasn't even sure why she was resisting. Acknowledging the bruises wouldn't make it any more real. She already knew she'd almost been raped. It was a solemn reminder of just how badly things could have gone for her with Convict if he were a different man.

Callused fingers pressed gently against her neck, an almost caress. "Fucking bastard." Unlike his touch, Convict's words were a sharp, dangerous growl. "Does it hurt a lot?"

"Not so much anymore." Actually, with him touching her, it felt pretty damn good.

He bent down and reached into his pack. The loss of his warmth sent a chill spiraling through her.

"Let me see those palms." He'd tucked a dark grey bottle under his arm.

She held out her hands without hesitation.

Now that he'd begun, she was ashamed to say she was enjoying it. She couldn't think of the last time someone had taken care of her like this. As the eldest, it had always been up to her to do the care taking.

Convict leaned over to examine her hands, his breath a warm caress against her neck. "There are some bad scratches." His touch was light, but firm as he rubbed a clear substance into her palms. It tingled, but didn't sting, and had the faint odor of flowers.

"What is that?" Her words were a bit slurred. Between the draining of her adrenaline and the rhythmic steady touch of his warm hands, she was being lulled into a very relaxed state.

He shrugged. "Doesn't have a name. I discovered it by accident. If you cut the leaves of a long spiky plant that grows in the Oasis, this stuff oozes out. It's great for healing cuts and preventing infections."

"You really are amazing."

His hand stilled. "I think you might be in shock."

She stared in stunned silence. "Did you just make a joke?"

"I don't know. Maybe." His lips tilted up in an almost half-smile. "It's been a while."

She smiled back, an answering giddy grin in celebration of survival. Of the fact that she and Convict were still alive. That they were here with one another in spite of everything Dragath25 kept throwing at them.

The surge of relief lasted all of five seconds.

Her grin crumpled. A sob escaped. The roiling emotions inside swinging back the other direction. She couldn't stand it another minute. She needed to feel his strength. Wipe away the horror of her attack. "Will you hold me? Please."

Without hesitation, his arms closed around her, the bottle under his arm dropping to the ground.

"It's okay, Bella." He hauled her close, his chin resting on the top of her head, her body cradled against his solid chest as she'd been craving all along. "You're safe."

Full on crying now, she wrapped her arms around him, too, curling into his strength, inhaling deeply. Letting the smell of him—of security and power and warm male—seep into her bones and soothe. "These past few days have been a lot to take in." She felt the need to try and explain.

"I know." The steady, soothing caress of his palm continued up and down her back. "I've seen grown men cry like a baby upon arrival. You're tougher than any of them."

She hid a shaky smile. Who knew her convict could be so sweet?

"I'm sorry I didn't stay where you said." She whispered the words to his chest. "I know how badly you must want to yell at me about that and I appreciate you holding off."

His hand stilled. "We'll have to talk about it some time."

"Just not right now."

"Agreed." His hands resumed their slow glide. And with every gentle pass of his hand, a little bit more of herself returned. She'd had a scare, yes. But she was fine. She was better than fine, in fact. She was alive. Safe. In the arms of a man who'd stood up for her as no one had in a long time. She'd forgotten what it was like to have someone in her corner.

Her uncertainty over staying with him slipped away. For the time being, this was exactly where she wanted to be. She'd deal with the consequences another day.

"Thank you for what you did today." Done with clinging, she brushed her lips against his chest, right across his heart.

He sucked in a breath.

She hid a watery smile. Such power to know she could have an effect on such a strong, stoic man.

"You saved me." She kissed his chest again. "You saved my colleagues." Another kiss.

"I didn't do it for them." His voice had dropped to that low rumble she'd come to associate with unbelievable pleasure.

"It was still incredibly brave." She traced her tongue over one flat nipple reveling in the way it tightened in her mouth. "I know you said not to call you a hero, but I can't help it. That's what you are to me."

He drew back as far as his hold would allow, his eyes haunted. "I'm no hero."

She had no interest in arguing. Her hands slid down the hard planes of his stomach to cup his thickening cock. "Whoever you are, whatever you are, I'm glad you're here with me."

He let out a low groan, but he didn't lean in to her touch. "I'm…I'm still messed up inside." His gaze shifted from hers. "On edge. We should wait. I… I don't think I can be gentle."

That damn stinging returned to her eyes. "I don't want gentle." Though the fact that he was willing to hold off for her touched her all over again. "I want you. I want what you've given me these last few days." Confident once more, she pressed butterfly kisses along his collarbone and throat while her hand stroked his hardening length. "I want you to take me like you did that first time. And then the next. And the next. I want to scream and writhe and beg."

She paused, awareness dawning. "It wasn't until I crashed on this planet and met you that I learned what pleasure was." *What it was like to be touched as if I mattered.* "Between scratching and clawing to feed my family, I'd forgotten such things were even allowed." She ran her tongue along the firm line of his jaw. "You reminded me of that, Convict. I don't want to forget. Especially now." She didn't want to be afraid to feel. Especially not for such an incredible man.

His nostrils flared. "Call me Caine."

"Caine?" The word tasted strange on her tongue. "Is that your name?"

"It was."

Several heartbeats passed in silence while she found her voice.

"It suits," she got out at last, feeling she'd won the greatest of prizes. "Touch me, *Caine*."

At the sound of his name, he froze. Then, with a ravenous growl, his mouth was skimming over her throat, making her moan, while his hands roamed everywhere. Marking her. Claiming her. Pleasuring her.

He'd said he couldn't be gentle, but his touch was whisper soft. Making her feel clean once again. Safe. Cherished. Closer to another human being than she'd ever felt in her life. Proving once again there was beauty to be found at the unlikeliest of times, in the unlikeliest of places, with the unlikeliest of men.

Caine's heart gave a little thump. It felt weird to hear her call him by his real name. But he couldn't deny he liked it. A lot more than he'd thought he would.

He wasn't even sure why he'd told her. Except he suddenly couldn't stand her calling him Convict. Not when it put him in the same category as the animal who'd hurt her.

A fast death had been too good for the bastard. But he hadn't wanted to upset his fighter girl any more than she already was.

Last time he'd killed, it had been methodical and deliberate and driven by the grim determination that it needed to be done, that an obligation was owed. Not this time. There'd been no careful logic, no sense of a debt due. No, this time the urge to kill had been far more primal. More instinctive. A predator protecting what was his.

Somehow, in the space of a few days, his fighter girl had moved from being a convenience to something far more.

Which wasn't smart. Wanting someone was one thing. But needing someone was altogether different.

He'd learned long ago to avoid the latter.

"Come inside me." Her voice was low and hoarse, her hand guiding his to her wet center. Refusing his retreat. Making it impossible for him to keep his distance. "I don't want to wait anymore. It won't be enough until I feel you deep inside."

On a groan, he let her set the pace. Let her fumble with his covering and pull out his cock. Let her rub herself against his tip while she moaned, her throat tipping back.

It only made him harder.

She was amazing. Allowing nothing to keep her down, mar her spirit. She always found a way to fight back. Truth be told, she humbled him.

"Caine." Her breathy use of his name made him groan out loud. He fucking loved hearing it on her lips. "Come in me. Now."

Grabbing her ass, he lifted her and thrust inside her warm heat. And found calm for the first time since he'd seen her being attacked. She was with him. She was safe.

But he couldn't screw up again. He had to double his vigilance. Make sure he didn't repeat the mistakes of his past.

Stilling inside her, he gripped her chin. "Starting tomorrow, you learn defensive moves that can help you get away from an attacker."

"Okay." Her eyes were already half-lidded, her pupils wide. He wasn't even sure she'd fully heard him.

"You'll learn to read the signs for approaching bad weather and the best places to look for shelter."

"Mmmm." She clenched her inner muscles in a clear sign of impatience. "Talk...later."

He stifled a groan. Forced himself to remain focused. "You'll learn the predators here and how to avoid them or you won't go outside."

Blinking slowly, she considered him for a long moment, those grass green eyes slicing right through his darkness. Then she surprised him. She leaned forward and kissed the skin right over his heart. Just like she'd done before. "There *is* honor on Dragath25. And selflessness, too. Thank you, Caine. For everything."

The place where she'd kissed him burned as if he'd been seared. His heart slamming against his ribs as if he'd run a mile.

Suddenly, there was no more ability to hold back. He sank deep inside, watching her beautiful, knowing eyes shut as pleasure gripped her and she moved easily with his fierce pace. As if they were made for one another.

She really did think he was one of the good guys—and damn him, but he wanted to be that for her. Even if it was too late. Even if what had happened with his wife had made that impossible.

But somehow, when he was deep inside his fighter girl like this, her legs wrapped around his waist, her full breasts rubbing against his chest, he didn't care how stupid it was. He wanted to be her everything. He wanted to be her hero forever.

Which, like it or not, meant letting her go.

The realization sliced straight through his chest like a rusty blade. One of these days soon, there'd be no more touches. No more palms laced together, her slender fingers anchoring him, soothing him. No more soft silk beneath his fingertips or breathy moans in his ear or watching her eyes light up with awe when he showed her a new location of plants and trees.

It would all come to an end just like he'd always known it would.

Because even with his fighter girl's impressive spirit, she'd never survive long on Dragath25. Not with 225's pack on her trail. Today had driven that home.

"Everything okay?" Her concerned tone slapped him back to the present.

He hadn't realized he'd stopped moving.

"Sure, fighter girl." He lifted her higher, shifting the angle so his palm could slide down her belly to play with her clit. "Everything is just the way it should be."

He wasn't one of the good guys, and he couldn't keep her forever, but he could do something right with what he had left of his life. He could do whatever it took to get her safely back on that rescue shuttle and able to save the precious Earth she was so keen to protect. He could, when the time came, let her go—and deal with whatever 225 threw his way.

But not a minute before he had to.

Because, yes, he was a selfish bastard. But also because he knew deep in his bones he was her best chance of staying alive until the rescue crew arrived.

He hadn't been able to save his wife, but he would safeguard Bella.

And watching her come apart, her skin flushed, her tits jiggling up and down as she rode him hard, well,…in the meantime that was a hell of a consolation prize. One he'd be replaying over and over when she was back where she belonged and he was alone again.

CHAPTER ELEVEN

Bella's shoulder hit the ground first, her teeth vibrating inside her skull.

Exhausted, sweaty, her muscles screaming, she flopped onto her back and surveyed the rust-colored cave ceiling overhead. It was as austere as the rest of Caine's home.

She'd had little chance to look around when they'd arrived in near darkness late last night, her body exhausted from the trek and the day's events, her eyes barely able to stay open.

But from what she could tell in the light of day, she hadn't missed much. Beyond the weapon arena she was currently lying in, there was a kitchen area with a fire pit and stocks of food and water and a separate area with a bed. A surprisingly comfy bed she wished she was still in.

Supposedly, there was a warm spring in one of the back caverns, but she hadn't seen any evidence of it yet. Caine had been too intent on getting going with her training. While she might not be accountable for every waking movement as she had been under Council protocol, her current situation suddenly didn't feel too different.

Truth be told, the Caine who faced her now appeared almost as rigid. Much like his home. Everything in his place was neat and orderly and very utilitarian. There was nothing that didn't serve a purpose. Nothing that suggested frivolity or fun. Nothing that indicated what the hell he'd been doing for the last eight years besides trying to survive.

"I really thought I had you that time." It wasn't true, but if she said it often enough, maybe he'd believe she was actually improving and let her take a break. She hadn't realized he'd be quite this intense about her training.

"Again." Without warning, Caine grabbed her wrist and lifted her to her feet, his scowl firmly in place. She'd thought yesterday had brought them closer, but apparently, that had been a one-day scenario, at least on his part. Because whatever tenderness he'd shown after yesterday's attack was nowhere to be found today. In its place was a guarded reserve she didn't welcome or understand.

Unless they were having sex. Then she sensed the same desperation he'd shown when they first met. In fact, when she'd woken up early this morning, he'd fucked her like he might never again. Then he'd done it three more times. Her legs were still rubbery.

She took a deep breath and reminded herself not to jump to conclusions. After all, he'd been on his own a long time. They had limited time to train. He was used to a hard way of life. Not to mention it might take some time for him to grow accustomed to having someone else under foot all the time.

The list of justifications went on and on. Plus, it was no small thing that he was pushing her so she could defend herself against monsters like the one she'd encountered yesterday—and she wanted that, too. Wanted to be able to defend against anything that might come her way. Especially since she hadn't given up on saving the approaching Council rescue shuttle and finding a way to return to Earth.

"Remember to watch your left. You're dropping it every time." He bent into a crouch, the flickering light from the glow torches on the walls dancing off the carved muscles of his stomach highlighting every mouthwatering shift and flex. His sexy happy trail disappearing beneath the waistband of a pair of faded camo pants that sat low on his hips. Honestly, the man was temptation itself.

She didn't know if the shift from the loincloth was a laundry issue or a sign he was embracing more of the man he'd once been, but she was taking it as a good omen.

He'd given her a new faded t-shirt to wear as well. It was as roomy as the last, but free of dust and dirt and hung to her knees—which was good since she still had no underwear. Outside, wind and dust battered at the thick cave walls, as loud as a shuttle engine.

The dust storm, which had started early this morning, had made it impossible for them to head out to warn her crew about 225 and the trackers. A situation that had worried her until Caine pointed out 225's men were trapped as well.

Her breath left her in a rush as her feet swept out from under her.

Caine had come at her while she was lost in thought. She braced herself for a jarring landing. But like last time, he caught her at the last minute, slowing her decent so she landed with one tenth the force. Still, her shoulder smarted.

"You're not paying attention," he barked. "You need to stay on guard. Alert. Any distraction can get you killed."

Still on her back, she looked up to find him glowering down at her, his arms crossed over his wide chest. Even with that frown, he was beautiful. His chiseled cheekbones and square jaw pure masculinity. His bronzed skin covered in ropey muscle after muscle. The crisscross of scars across his body proved him every inch the warrior. Still, there was no give in him at all. In his body. In his demeanor. In his approach.

Her determination to be optimistic wavered. Could he already regret bringing her to his home?

Maybe that wouldn't have bothered her if she still thought of him as only a short-term necessity to endure. But her feelings had been shifting, little by little—perhaps even from the moment he'd first touched her with that look of awe—and after yesterday, they'd solidified. Her desire to please him increasingly prompted by far more than the instinct to survive and the deal they'd made.

He might be a Dragath25 criminal; he might have done awful things in his past, but that wasn't who he was with her.

All her life, she'd been around people—crowded into tight spaces to optimize scarce resources and space—but even so, she'd been alone. Isolated by her responsibilities and her ambition. Sure, she'd dated a few men here and there and indulged in some quick, perfunctory sex when her needs became too great, but none of those affairs had ever lasted beyond a few weeks. None had ever been worth risking her position and allowing herself to get close.

But Caine was different. She'd *had* to depend on him or die, and in the process, she was pretty certain she'd opened herself up to him as she never had to anyone else. It made her feel ripped wide open and...vulnerable.... maybe, embarrassingly enough, even a little insecure.

He mattered to her. She wanted to matter to him as well.

Which made his aloofness this morning all the more troubling.

Pushing onto her elbows, she studied him, searching for any clues to what he was thinking. "Let's take a break. Maybe talk? I know so little—"

"No breaks."

She was flying through the air to land on her feet in the next instant.

"Stop doing that." She shook off his hold. "I can get up myself."

He raised an eyebrow. "But can you stay up?"

"This time you're going down, smart ass." Irritated, she went into her own crouch, murmuring to herself. "Left hand by the face. Weight on balls of the feet. Grab his wrist, turn, use his momentum...."

Then he was coming at her and there was no more time to think. Just act.

Her shoulder met the ground again. "That's it." She rolled to sit, her elbow propped on her knees. Yes, she wanted to learn to defend herself, but she needed time to clear her head. "You've pummeled me enough for the morning. I need a rest."

A muscle jumped in his jaw. "You think 225's men are going to go easy on you?" He stalked forward until their bare feet were touching. "I can't be around every minute." His voice was rough with tension. His features taut. "Come on, Gwen, at least make a god damn effort."

Her ears twitched, every nerve going on alert. "Gwen? Who's Gwen?"

His expression blanked. "Don't worry about it." He flowed back into his offensive stance as if nothing had happened. "Let's get back to it, fighter girl. Keep your weight evenly distributed. You can do this."

She didn't move.

For some stupid reason, she'd never considered he might have a woman in his life. Someone he missed. Someone he thought of every time he was fucking her.

"My name is Bella. Not fighter girl." It was suddenly important that he call her that. That she hear *her* name on his lips.

"What?"

"I'd like you to call me Bella."

His lips flat-lined. "You think it makes a difference what I call you?"

"You should at least know the name of the woman you're currently fucking."

He stretched to his full, intimidating height, tense silence filling the room; ominous, heavy.

Her heart skittered inside her chest, all her silly, happily-ever-after imaginings crumbling to dust.

"You know what, Bella?" he said at last, her name sounding almost like a curse. "You were right before. We could both use a break."

From training? Or the deal? She was too afraid to ask for fear she wouldn't like the answer. Instead, she watched in silence as he stalked to the kitchen area and grabbed a cup of water. And even though she could see his Adam's apple sliding up and down as he drank deep, even though she could see the sexy curve of his lip as he held the cup to his mouth, he could have been a solar system away with the length of the distance he'd put between them.

CHAPTER TWELVE

"What are you working on?" Tired of the impasse that had kept them in separate corners of the cave for the last hour, Bella crossed to where Caine was hunched over a mish-mash collection of colorful, frayed wires and beat up circuits. It must have taken years to accumulate it all.

"Not much." He didn't look up.

"Is that the start of an engine for some kind of space ship?"

He snorted.

Yes, that's what she'd thought, but a girl could hope. "What is it then?"

"Just a heap of trash now."

"And when it's done?"

There was a long pause. The pounding of the storm debris against the cave walls only made the quiet inside more acute.

"Fine." She turned away, her voice tight and sharp. "We don't have to talk at all. Silence is good, too."

A hand wrapped around her ankle, checking her in place.

"I've had eight years of silence, Bella." This time her name held no anger. "I don't need anymore."

Guilt settled low in her stomach. She might have been on her own her whole life, but Caine had been truly alone. No siblings to offer a smile or a hug. No colleagues with which to discuss the latest theories. No bunkmates to commiserate with over a late night of smuggled-in banned drinks.

What right did she have to begrudge him memories of people from his past? Or take his reserve personally? Maybe she would never matter to him like he did to her, but they could still co-exist. She swallowed past the lump in her throat and pretended her chest didn't hurt.

"Okay." She plopped down on the floor beside him, her own form of olive branch. "Can I help?" She gestured toward his project.

"Sure." He handed her a couple unattached wires. "See if you can peel away the burnt coating. It's no good anymore, but the wire beneath could still be useful."

She got to work. Sitting side by side, working in tandem, was...relaxing. Peaceful. Washing away the last of the tension between them. At his urging, she told him about her childhood, her brother and sister, and her work. Though he didn't say much, she did manage to learn he'd grown up on one of the rare working farms still in existence twenty years ago and that he'd traveled to a heck of a lot more places on Earth than she'd ever been.

It was nice simply being together. Learning his habits. The way his brow drew down when he was concentrating. The way he rubbed at the scar on his right thumb when he was listening to her stories, a faint smile on his gorgeous face.

A while later, she got up to get some water. Caine kept working away. His project still resembling nothing she could identify.

"Are you sure that's not a space ship engine that can fly us out of here?"

He took the water she proffered, his throat muscles moving up and down as he took a long drink. "Still dreaming of us both getting out of here, fighter gi—ah, Bella?"

"Of course. The good guys always win in the end," she joked, appreciative he'd made an effort to use her name.

"Good guys, huh?" He looked hard at the jumble of wires. "What if I told you when it's done it will be something similar to the equipment used by 225's pack to override your shuttle's computers?"

"The thing that caused us to crash?" She suddenly didn't even like looking at the contraption. It felt ominous. And deadly.

He ran his hand over one of the wires. "Exactly."

"Why would you make something like that?" Her voice came out shriller than intended, memories of the crash making her throat go tight.

His fingers stilled. "Why do you think?"

"I don't know, but I'm certain it's not for the same purpose used by 225. You're not a killer."

"I'm not?" The deliberate way he placed his work onto the ground and unfolded to stand above her proved they'd waded back into dangerous territory. "I killed that tracker."

"That was different."

"Was it? A life gets taken all the same."

She stood, trying to lessen the space between them. "If you hadn't killed those men, they would have killed us. You were acting in self-defense."

"I haven't always." His admission was a harsh whisper. "You say I'm some kind of good guy, but these hands that have been all over you? That have been deep inside your pussy and worked you good? These hands you're thinking can easily tag along when you fly away from Dragath25? These are killer hands, fighter girl." He held them out in front of him, curling them into fists, making the web of milky white scars stand out all the more against his bronze skin. "There's no washing that away. Or pretending otherwise. No matter what."

"People can change," she said a little desperately, not sure how they'd ended up here. Or why he kept deliberately trying to push her away. "People can make mistakes and then fix them and move on."

He took a step closer, his voice a low, menacing rumble. "What if I don't think I made a mistake? What if I'd do the same thing that put me here over and over again?"

She took a step back, the certainty in his voice, in his guilt, in his conviction that he wasn't worth saving, raising her own doubts. "I don't...." She honestly wasn't sure how to respond, but there was one thing she did know for sure. "Whatever happened in the past, you can't use that device to bring down another shuttle. That would make you a monster."

His hands fisted by his side. "I'm going for some air." He stalked toward the door.

"But there's a dust storm. You can't go out in that."

"It's settling now."

She couldn't let this drop. She couldn't let him dodge this issue because she feared his disapproval or worse. "I won't let you use this thing on another shuttle like mine."

He paused with his hand on the door handle, his back still to her. "People can change, huh?"

"Yes." Relief whispered through her. Maybe she'd reached him after all.

"You sure you believe that, fighter girl?" He looked over his shoulder, his jaw tight. "Because I never said I built that device intending to bring down a shuttle."

She opened her mouth to respond. Nothing came out.

"That kind of stuff is for sadists like 225 and his pack," he continued. "I might be a killer and a criminal, but I'm not like them. I planned on using my jammer to seize control of one of the unmanned droids that dump trash twice a year. More recently though, I was trying to get it to jam a device similar to itself so we could stop 225, save your precious search and rescue team, and get you the hell off Dragath25."

He shut the door firmly behind him.

It didn't escape her notice he'd only mentioned her departure.

Or that the first time the tables were turned and he'd needed her to be his hero—to believe in him no matter what—she'd failed.

CHAPTER THIRTEEN

"I'll be back as soon as I can." Breathing hard, Caine wedged the last of the boulders into place in front of the door.

Bella tried to keep her worry at bay. The storm had indeed settled down. But the tempest between her and Caine remained. He hadn't gone far when he left, only just outside the cave entrance, but he'd stayed there a long while. He'd come inside caked in red dust only to inform her the weather had improved enough for him to go warn her colleagues. Then he started dragging in boulders the size of small planets.

It was clear he didn't want to talk about what had happened before.

"Are you sure I can't go with you?" She trailed in his wake, the distance between them as vast as ever. "You're going to have a hard time getting them to listen without me there."

"I'll do my best." He strapped a small knife to the pocket of his camo pants and seized his spear. Even before their argument, he'd been immoveable in his refusal to take her. She got it. She'd only slow him down when speed was of the essence. Still, she hated the idea that he was off to risk himself without her to watch his back. More so when things were so uneasy between them.

"If for some reason I can't make it back in a few hours," he said, "there are additional glow sticks in the third drawer from the top. There's also enough dried food in the kitchen to last a lifetime."

"But you'll be back way before a lifetime, I'm sure." Her joke fell flat, her voice a little uncertain even to her own ears.

He shoved a container of dried food into his pack. "Right. But just in case." He still hadn't looked up. "Remember what I told you. Don't go outside for any reason."

She glanced at the huge pile of boulders that now barricaded the door. "I don't think that will be a problem."

He paused in his packing. "It better not be." He finally looked at her, the lines around his eyes tight with tension. To her surprise, his gaze was dark with concern. No anger in sight. "Don't forget to put more of that salve on your bruises. It's easy to get an infection here. And don't venture into the back caverns while I'm not here. You could get lost or slip."

Buoyed by his concern, she grabbed his arm, his bicep so big she could barely wrap her hand around half. "I'm sorry about before."

"It's fine."

"No. It's not. I shouldn't have assumed you intended to use your invention to crash a manned shuttle. I don't...I don't know much about your past, but I do know you've been nothing but fair and patient and generous since we met. Fear just got the best of me for a minute. It won't happen again."

He nodded, his expression as unreadable as ever. "Okay."

Not the most satisfying of responses.

"I think...I think I'm not the best at this whole depending on someone else thing. It's making me act stupid." She darted a quick glance his way.

She thought he might smile. Instead, he let out a slow, shuddering breath. "Look, Bella, it's really okay. This is new territory for both of us. We'll figure it out."

Also not exactly the response for which she'd hoped. His resigned tone only made her more terrified that he sensed her growing feelings and wasn't sure how to let her down easy. Was he, horror of all horrors, simply being nice? Or wishing even now it was that Gwen person standing next to him?

"I don't want to be a burden." She took a deep breath and forced the words out. "If you want me gone by the time you return, just say it."

Everything inside Caine stilled. "What did you say?"

"I want you to tell me if you've tired of our deal and you want me gone." Her gaze shifted from his. "It's alright if you do. Just tell me straight out."

It took all his control to keep his voice measured. "I want you here."

"You say that," she said, doubt clear in her tone, "but—"

"No but. That's the way things are."

She might make things hard, she might awaken memories and heroic impulses better left dead and buried, but it didn't matter. He wasn't letting her go until he had to.

She nodded, slowly, as if she still wasn't convinced.

He knew things weren't going like she'd hoped, but they'd iron it out in time. Get used to each other's sore spots. He'd figure out how to get his head on straight. How to staunch the war within that one minute had him wanting to fuck her so hard and deep she permanently cleaved to his side, and the next minute wanting to push her far enough away that he wouldn't even notice when he had to let her go.

In the meantime, he'd make damn sure not to say Gwen's name again. Because he knew without a doubt that his mention of Gwen was what had set his fighter girl off, got her worrying about his past, thinking of him all over again as a Dragath25 criminal, wondering if she could trust him, making her reconsider their deal.

"I'm the best one to protect you," he reminded her, not too proud to use the one card he knew he still held.

"I'm sure of that," she agreed quickly. Too quickly. Her fingers worrying at the hem of her shirt.

Stymied, he ran a hand over the soft fuzz on his head. He was reluctant to leave and yet unsure what to say next. He could tell she wanted something more from him, but he wasn't interested in rehashing his past—he wanted her to keep looking at him with respect, after all.

Plus, talking about all of that only made him stupid, only made his heart pound and his throat close. Post-traumatic stress, one prison doc had said. Guilt decreed another. Whatever the hell it was, he couldn't afford to let that kind of emotion distract him now. He had to remain focused.

"I have to go." But unable to resist, he pulled her close, drawing in the sweet scent of her, memorizing the feel of her softness against him. "I want to be back before the next dust storm hits." The thought of her alone for a few hours was hard enough. He wasn't about to let a storm keep him away for more than that. "When I come back, we'll take a trip to the Oasis. You can take samples. Measurements. We can even swim in the lake if you like."

He held his breath.

It felt like hours, but eventually she leaned into him, her body a little stiff, but her arms still wrapped around his neck, her big green eyes bright with the kind of hesitant warmth that made him feel they'd be all right if he could just keep it together. He wanted whatever time he had left with her to be good.

"I'd love that. Thanks." She rose on tiptoe and kissed his jaw, another good sign. "If Pogue and the others won't listen, don't stay around and try to convince them, okay? We'll figure something else out. Just…just be safe."

He tried to take away the worry. "I'll be back before you know it."

"Just don't take unnecessary risks."

His dark gaze bore into her. "Too late."

He could tell by her puzzled expression she didn't get it. Probably for the better. If she understood just how essential she'd become to his wellbeing, she might do something silly, like start talking again about redemption and how people could change, and try and convince him to come with her when he figured out how to make his jammer work in their favor. And as much as he wanted off this hellhole, he knew that wasn't possible. Not if he wanted the Council to let her off this planet alive. They'd never let him set foot on that shuttle, much less Earth, and he'd only be putting her in more danger if he tried.

Knowing he couldn't delay any longer, he stepped back, took one more good look at her...and vaulted upward, catching the rim of the window. Without too much effort, he swung his legs up and slid through, falling for a good few seconds before his boots slammed into the ground.

He looked up to see the top of her blonde head and two gorgeous worried eyes peering down. "You okay?"

"Fine. Careful on that table." He didn't like the idea of her up on that rickety thing. Hell, he didn't like the idea of any of this. It would be so easy—so fucking easy—for her to get killed while he was away. "Board up the window like we planned. I won't leave until I'm sure it's done."

Finding out Gwen had been screwing around on him had been bad, but he'd understood. They'd been young and dumb and known each other for less than six months when they got married. And while they'd definitely cared about each other, there'd been signs from the start that they weren't compatible for the long run. For all her good traits—and there'd been plenty—Gwen had turned out to be less comfortable with standing on her own than they'd both expected. She'd grown increasingly resentful of every deployment and, eventually, found someone else who could take care of her in his absence.

Truth be told, once his ego had adjusted, he'd been almost relieved. He'd wanted her to be happy and he'd been willing to wish her well. Until he heard who she'd hooked up with. A married asshole Councilman from their District who lived like a king while the rest of the population got by on limited rations and supplies. Word was her new lover was extremely corrupt and a bad man to cross. Caine had warned Gwen, but she hadn't listened. She'd wanted the attention, the easy life, the security too much. And he hadn't done enough to guard her from herself.

In the end, it had cost them both everything.

He had no intention of making the same mistakes with his fighter girl.

Sweat rolled down his back as he waited for her to give the all-clear sign. His mind pictured her going through the instructions he'd laid out. First, she'd shut and bolt the wooden slats, and then, one big rock at a time, heft them into place in front of the window until she'd built a mini version of the same kind of barricade he'd placed in front of the door. No tigos would be able to get in. No 225 rapist, either.

"It's done," she shouted, her voice muffled by the barriers. "Good luck. I'll be here when you get back."

She better fucking be.

CHAPTER FOURTEEN

Bella poked her finger into the dirt, making a nice air pocket for one of the seedlings she'd found stuck to the bottom of her boot. Her gaze traveled to the two other pots she'd planted with seeds from Caine's food supply. Then to the failure of a cup she'd tried to whittle for herself with one of Caine's knives and some spare wood.

She was running out of ways to distract herself.

With an impatient sigh, she headed to the kitchen area to trickle some water over her hands and stir the mix of grains and meat she'd decided to try and prepare after watching Caine this morning. Cooking over a bunch of burning rocks wasn't anything like the Academy's instant synthetic processor, but she was relieved to find it smelled delicious. If it tasted half as good, she'd be pleased with her first effort. Hopefully, Caine would be, too.

He'd said he wanted her here, and she was accepting that. No second guessing. No giving into silly insecurities. No obsessing about this Gwen person or his crimes. Or making more of what was between her and Caine than there was. She had calculated there were at least five more days minimum until the rescue shuttle arrived, and if Caine's trip was successful, she was determined to spend them with him. To simply enjoy the present for as long as she could.

Or she would. Once Caine returned. She was done trying to make the best of her alone time. She wanted him back. She needed to know he was safe.

A faint sound had her hopping up on the table, spear in hand, the dry stale air from outside hitting her square in the face. Yes, she'd taken down the barricade in front of the window and opened the slats a while ago.

She didn't like small, closed spaces. Never had. And the sense that she was in a tomb had stayed with her until she'd knocked down the rocks, ripped open the slats, and sucked down some fresh air. Hot as it was, vulnerable as it made her, it had still felt glorious.

Though the act itself had been pure anxious impulse, she'd reasoned since that the space was so small whatever came through would have to come single file and slowly, too. Spear raised high, she was ready for any unwelcomed guest.

Her gaze scanned the perimeter. Nothing. She tapped a solemn beat against the stone.

And then, as if she'd willed him into appearing, Caine's dark head and wide shoulders appeared on the path, his spear and backpack slung around his back, his familiar graceful, commanding stride stealing her breath.

It seemed to take forever for him to reach the cave. Longer still for his black boots and long legs to slide through the window.

He landed in a crouch on the floor.

"You're back!" Setting the spear against the wall, she rushed forward, relief making her giddy. "You were gone so long. Did everything go okay?"

"The window wasn't bolted."

She froze, the arms that had been about to envelop him dropping back to her sides. "I was growing worried about you." Probably best not to mention it had been open far longer than that.

"All the more reason to keep it shut."

She studied him. He looked tense, but good. No new scratches or bruises. But there was something lurking just beneath the surface of his skin that raised goose bumps on her flesh. He looked…haunted.

"I needed some air," she said at last.

"You told me you'd keep it shut." His pack dropped to the ground, making her jump. "If I can't trust you to keep your word, how can I leave you to get things done?"

Definitely not the homecoming she'd imagined.

"I'm fine." She spread her arms wide. She needed him to stop treating her as if she were so fragile. "In fact, I'm better than fine. I was by myself. For the first time in my life. In a small, dark space—which I don't always like. And I handled it far better than I suspected I would. Even better, you're back, safe and sound. We should be celebrating."

"I didn't know you were claustrophobic. You should have told me."

"I handled it."

He blew out a breath. "Which is great, but you can't take unnecessary risks."

"You're right." Sensing he was softening, she put her hand on his arm. "I'll be more careful. But try and remember I really am stronger than I look. Now, put me out of my misery and tell me what happened. Were you able to talk with my colleagues? Is everyone okay?"

His scowl deepened. "Those idiot soldiers of yours have been venturing farther and farther from the campsite, leaving an easy trail for any trackers to follow. I cleaned up their trail, but I won't be able to keep their camp site hidden forever, especially without their cooperation."

Her selfish plans for some time with Caine crumbled. "So they wouldn't listen?"

"Listen?" he snorted. "They shot at me the instant I showed myself."

She scanned him once more to make sure he was unharmed. "I'm so sorry."

"I expected nothing less."

"I'll go next time. Pogue may not listen, but Winthrop and Ava will."

"You're not going anywhere near there. But don't be so sure it would make a difference. That friend of yours is stubborn."

So much for her insistence he remember her capability. "You spoke with her?"

"I knew you'd be worried. It was easy enough to sneak in to camp and find her."

Her stomach turned at the risk he'd taken. If Pogue or the other soldiers had caught him, they would have killed him on sight.

"You told me you wouldn't take such risks," she accused.

His gaze shifted to the window. "I guess we both made promises we didn't keep."

Damn it. She hadn't realized he'd care so much about a silly window. But then again, she'd never been the cowering kind. It was better he learned that now. If he was going to come to see her as anything more than a fuck toy, it had better be the real her.

Still, she left it alone for now. There were more pressing concerns. "What did Ava say? Is she holding up?"

"Her leg is still bothering her, and it doesn't look like she's eating or drinking enough, but she's hanging in there. She was worried about you." He scooped up his pack and started unpacking, returning every tool and carton to its precise place. "She was relieved when I told her you were safe."

"She's a good person. I hate to think of her in such a precarious position."

"I tried to get her to come with me, but she refused."

Her chest squeezed tight, touched he would so willing to take on responsibility for another.

"Why wouldn't she come? Do you think she thought it was a trick?"

"I asked her the same thing. She said she believed me." He grew very interested in examining one of her dirt samples. "Said she'd seen the way I looked as I carried you away from the saybak. That it was clear I'd never hurt you. That I'd do whatever it took to protect you."

Bella's heart stuttered a beat. Ava had seen the same thing she did. Caine was a good man. The only trouble with a champion, though, was you didn't know if their urge to protect was because that's just what they did or because they thought you were special.

He set the dirt sample down. "She said to tell you she was sorry, but she couldn't come now. She said you'd understand. Their team lost two more soldiers yesterday. One to the dust storm. The other to some kind of food poisoning. Tensions are running high, and she's worried about your buddy Winthrop."

"Is he dying?" Guilt speared through her. She never should have left them.

"He's fine." A hard edge had entered Caine's voice.

She pretended not to notice. "Then why is Ava worried?"

"Winthrop and Pogue aren't getting along. Each blames the other for your disappearance, and with every passing minute, Pogue's growing more resentful of Winthrop's orders. There's a definite leadership struggle underway, and Ava isn't sure how much longer Winthrop's influence will last or what Pogue will do if the rescue team doesn't show up soon."

"All the more reason for her to get as far away from Pogue as possible." But she understood Ava's reluctance to leave what seemed safe. Bella herself had been willing to forgive far too much when it came to Winthrop and Pogue simply because they were familiar. Looking back now, she realized she'd been all too desperate to cling to the rules and order of Council life. No doubt a side effect of growing up in a society that demanded unquestionable adherence to the established hierarchical authority. It had taken Caine for her to see how clearly she'd placed her trust in the wrong men.

Unfortunately, her needs weren't the only one at stake here.

Bella ran a hand down her face, wishing for answers she didn't have. "Did you tell Ava about the rescuers?"

"Yes, but she doesn't believe it. She refuses to believe it." He let out a long sigh. "She just patted my hand and assured me I was mistaken. Said there'd been a lot of recent technological advances in shuttlecraft. That the rescue team knew what they were doing. That they would find a way to land. Then she got all sad...mumbled something about how escaping her family and the Council wouldn't be that easy."

Bella's eyebrow rose at that last comment. There was clearly far more to Ava's story, little of it good. "Can we just kidnap her?" 225's pack would find the campsite, eventually.

"No. Your soldiers have too many guns, and they're twitchy enough as it is. Spying on them from afar is risky enough."

She let out a long, slow breath, her chest tight. "Which is why I need to go back and tell them myself what's going on."

He stiffened. "You're not going back there."

"It isn't up to you." Still, worry skittered through her. He wasn't suggesting he would keep her against her will, was he? He'd been so adamant about her being the one to make the choice to keep their deal, she never once considered he wouldn't also allow her to sever the deal.

"It isn't?" He took a step closer. "We made a deal. You told me anything in return for keeping you safe. And I'm telling you you're not going back there. It's too dangerous."

She stood firm. "They're my colleagues."

"Are you forgetting what happened last time?" He plowed a hand through his short hair. "If not for that saybak, things would have gotten ugly."

"That was because you were with me. It won't happen when I'm alone."

"Alone?" he roared. "You want to go there alone? No way."

She must be crazy because, despite her annoyance over his highhandedness, his protectiveness warmed her. Comforted her, too. It would have been an easy out for him to agree. A quick and painless way to send her on her way and wash himself of an increasingly heavy burden. Instead, he was scowling and tense, his legs spread wide apart, barring her from the exit, proving that he really meant it when he said he wanted her to stay.

And God help her, but she didn't want to leave him just yet either. Truth be told, if it was just about her needs, she was almost certain she wouldn't have wanted to leave at all. She'd have preferred to find a way past his defenses. Learn his past. Relish the present. Turn his protectiveness into something deeper.

But burying her head in the sand was impossible.

"I'm sorry, Caine." She swallowed past the lump in her throat. "My colleagues need my help. And the fact is, we both know I can't stay here forever anyway." There. It was said. She held her breath, waiting for his reaction.

"Is this about this morning?" A muscle ticked in his jaw. "Because I told you. I want you to stay."

She raised her hand to touch him—and then fisted her palm by her thigh instead. "This...This isn't about that. It–it isn't about you and me at all."

He took a step closer, his chest heaving, red stamped across his carved cheekbones. "Are you sure about that? Are you sure you're not just running scared? Getting to know the real Dragath25 criminal and not liking what you find?"

No!" Her heart beat fast. Too fast. Making her wonder if there was any truth to his challenge. Not that she didn't like what she was finding. But that she liked it—him—too much. Too much to stay in something that felt all too temporary.

But that wasn't all of what was going on. She knew that, too. "It just feels wrong to be here when I should be helping my colleagues."

His nostrils flared, his eyes narrowing. "Colleagues? Or that Council Doctor?"

"Colleagues." She forced herself to say the rest of what needed to be said. "Plus, why not now? We both know I have to go back sometime soon. My brother and sister and all those left on Earth are depending on me to return, and staying near Winthrop is the only way that will happen."

Jaw clenched, Caine's gaze shifted away from hers, freezing when they landed on the heap of wires in the corner. "You want to help them? Stay and help me get the jammer running. Your Command Council Officer may be the key to drawing the rescue shuttle, but those soldiers will never make it within a hundred metrals of him if the jammer isn't operational."

"But you don't need me to work on—"

"I do." He still hadn't looked at her. "I do need you."

Her heart skittered and took flight. Could it be they weren't only talking about the jammer anymore?

"Give me a few days." His gaze slammed back into her, his expression unreadable again. "I'll see what I can do with the jammer, and in the meantime, I'll deliver a message from you to Ava. Maybe something written in your own hand will persuade her of the dangers. And I'll make sure you're back with him–," he swallowed hard, "–with Winthrop–when the time comes." He nodded once. "I'll get you home, Bella. I swear it."

Her. He'd get her home. Not the two of them.

She rubbed at her chest with the palm of her hand. "Okay." It was settled. Her worry put to rest. He'd take her back if and when the time came. So why did it feel as if her chest were being torn in two?

"Okay?" One eyebrow rose, some of the tension leaving his shoulders. "That's it?"

"I trust you, Caine. If you say you'll get me home, I know you will."

He nodded, his jaw still clenched tight.

Done fighting her instinct, she walked over and wrapped her arms around him—or, at least, around as much of him as she could, his hard chest as comforting and warm as ever. "Thank you for everything."

For an instant, he'd just stood there awkwardly, a little stiff, a lot unsure. Then his arms came around her and he gripped her tightly. "You're welcome." His voice was gruff.

She'd have given anything in that moment to know what he was thinking.

Was he secretly cursing the deal he'd made and the burdens of extra responsibility and risk it had heaped upon him? Or, like her, was he floored to discover that, if not for her worry over her siblings and the approaching rescue shuttle, she could stay in his arms forever and be happy?

CHAPTER FIFTEEN

The ripple of warm water against her shoulders soothed Bella's nerves.

While the rest of Caine's home might be sparse, this side chamber was indulgence itself: a patchwork of vivid emerald moss and red smooth rocks surrounding a small clear spring. It might not have the dramatic plants or pink lake of the Oasis, or the purple fruit and fan-shaped palms of the first cave Caine had taken her to, but it was equally lovely in its own quiet way. Even the melodic plinking of condensation slipping back into the water was calming.

Exactly what she needed right now.

She'd retreated here after a strained dinner. Sure, Caine had wolfed down the meal she'd made, praising her efforts while his jaw worked overtime pretending she hadn't overcooked the meat. And if she hadn't thought him a good guy before, that act of kindness alone would have told her everything.

But tension still vibrated between them. Questions about the future, worries about what would happen tomorrow, returning with a vengeance the moment she'd stepped out of his arms. She had to return home. That she knew. Even if the thought of leaving Caine here alone made her stomach twist and her throat close tight.

Sighing, she scooped up handfuls of water. The droplets slipping through her fingers no matter how hard she tried to hold them close. Just like Caine himself.

Her hands blurred. She blinked fast.

What she needed was some distance. Some perspective. Even if she could somehow convince Caine to come with her, what did she think would happen? That somehow things would work out between them? She would still be a junior scientist bound by Council rule to do whatever it took to keep her siblings fed and housed. Plus, she had no idea who was waiting for Caine back on Earth. Or anything about his past for that matter. What he'd done to end up on Dragath25. Who the hell Gwen was.

Maybe Ava was right. Maybe her dreams of a possible future between them were foolish. Maybe they were nothing more than desperate pipedreams based on the intensity of the moment.

Her fist hit the water surface, sending spray flying into her face.

"Am I interrupting?"

She swiveled around at the rough rumble of Caine's voice, her vision clearing as the water rolled down her face.

Her breath caught in her throat.

He stood on the bank above, one arm stretched above his head, his fingers tucked into a rocky ledge, his other hand behind his back.

It was a stance with forced casual written all over it. Still, it didn't matter. With his chest bare, his legs planted far apart, his pants dipping low on his hips, the position put every slab of mouthwatering sculpted muscle on display.

Her nipples grew hard, her blood heating. And from the slow, smoldering half-smirk that eased across his face, he knew exactly what looking at him did to her.

Maybe amazing sex was all they'd ever really have, but at least it was something.

"You're not interrupting at all." Purposely wading to the more shallow section, she brought the soap across her chest in a slow, deliberate caress. "I was just getting cleaned up."

His grip on the ledge tightened, his gaze tracking her every move. "You missed a spot." It was more a growl than a sentence.

She kept her smile to herself. The spring might soothe some of her worries, but only being in Caine's arms could make them all disappear for a while. "Hmmm. Care to help me get it?"

"Hell yes." He prowled forward. Only to stop short. "Uh, no."

She frowned. Caine wasn't one to hesitate. "If this is about what I said before about leaving—"

"No." He cut her off. "I know why you said it. And I may not like your plan, but I do admire the way you look out for your colleagues and your siblings." He took a deep breath. "This–this is something else." His hand came from behind his back. "I meant to give you these before."

Her chest went tight.

Clutched in his big hand was an explosion of color, a tangle of stems and petals in blue and purple and yellow and pink, some standing up straight while others drooped over his hand.

"Flowers." She blinked fast. "You brought me flowers?"

"Yea." He shuffled his feet. "They got a little crumpled in the pack." He shook his head. "I meant to give them to you right away, but I got distracted."

"They're beautiful." She waded forward, her arms outstretched, a corresponding riot of color exploding in her chest. "The best gift I've ever gotten." Actually, the only gift she'd ever gotten. "Where'd you find them?"

"Oasis. The purple ones grow near the banks while the pink and yellow are in the trees."

The picture of him scurrying around collecting flowers almost brought her to her knees. He'd done so much for her already. Kept her safe. Killed to protect her. And now this.

Forget distance. Forget perspective. Forget pretending to herself her heart wasn't involved. She was going to seize every moment she could, and somehow, some way, she was going to figure out a way to take Caine with her when she left Dragath25. Even if they weren't meant to be in the long run. Even if he dumped her the second they were back on Earth. Maybe she didn't know everything about his past or how this woman Gwen factored into his life, but she knew enough about him to know he didn't deserve to die alone on Dragath25. She was getting him off this hellhole and back to the kind of life a good man like him deserved. With or without his help.

She held out her hand. Slowly, he crouched at the edge of the ledge and handed them over. Cradling them like a child, careful not to let even one slip through her grasp, she lifted them to her nose and inhaled.

The fragrance was amazing. Floral. Sweet. Precious life, beauty, and hope all tangled together. Just like what she felt in Caine's arms.

"I want you here, Bella."

Her gaze flew to his.

"I know I've been a moody pain in the ass. I know I can sometimes get a little too intense about safety. I know I'm not the chattiest of guys. But none of that is any kind of reflection on my thinking about you." He cleared his throat. "I'm glad you're here." His gaze trailed from her eyes to her lips and back again. "I understand you have to go—eventually. But until that time comes, I want you here with me. Not just because I'm the best one to keep you safe. Or even because of the deal." He sucked down a deep breath. "Just...just because."

It was another incredible gift. And one she knew was all the more precious because it hadn't been easy for him to offer up.

"I want to be here." She looked up at him standing so beautiful and so alone on the rock above and her heart twisted. *Please, oh please, let me figure out a way to save him as well.* "Not just because you can keep me safe or because of our deal, but...but just...just because as well."

Maybe she should have said more. Maybe she should have admitted exactly how she felt. Or confessed her plans. But she couldn't. Not when the future was so uncertain between them.

"So we're okay?" His gaze had that hungry look again.

With a final deep inhale of their fragrance, she dipped the stems in the water and placed them gently a safe distance from the edge. "We're more than okay." She held out her arms again—this time for him. "Join me?"

In the next heartbeat, water splashed onto the bank, his chest warm and slick against her skin, his soaked pants slapping against her legs as he lifted her flush against him.

Laughing, she wrapped her legs around his waist and trusted him to keep her afloat. "Eager much?"

The droplets of water clinging to his long, spiky lashes only made his expression more intense. "I'm going to seize every second I've got."

That wiped the smile from her face. "So am I." Locking her gaze with his, she cradled his square jaw in her hands and brought their foreheads to touch. "Just because."

CHAPTER SIXTEEN

"I may never move again." Bella rolled off Caine's slick body, flopping onto her back to stare overhead at the lush canopy of the Oasis, her breathing still frantic from their latest bout of sex, her skin flushed from the mix of midday heat and arousal. The warm lake water lapped at her toes.

"Mmmm." He slipped his hand around her ass and slid her close enough to press fully against his side, hip to hip.

After five blissful days together, Caine still wasn't much of a talker, but he communicated his wants just fine.

"Thanks for bringing me here again today." She studied an unusual purple flowering vine high up in one of the trees, making a note to take a closer look when she regained the use of her legs. The flowers Caine had first given her were still her favorite, but she'd discovered quite a few other varieties since then, adding to her spectacular collection and her growing scientific understanding of the fragile environment.

"You're welcome." His fingers interlaced with hers, their palms pressing close. It had become a habit. One she cherished. "I like it here, too." His voice was roughened by sex and sleepiness. "Don't know why I never really hung out here before."

She hid a smile. She knew why. Until a few days ago, the man hadn't known the meaning of taking a break. He'd spent all waking minutes hunting, training, or working on the jammer. Was it no wonder he was wound so tight? Was it no wonder he'd forgotten there was more to life than simply surviving?

Sure, he'd been the first one to show her pleasure, to insist she could strive for more than pain and grim hard work, but his definition of where and how to seize such pleasure had been limited to sex. She'd had to show him right back that he was allowed the same opportunity—and that sex wasn't the only way to achieve it. Frankly, she was still working on that. He was proving far more stubborn than she.

It had taken all her coaxing to get him to relax even a little the first time they'd come to the Oasis. He'd watched the surrounding terrain like a hawk, spear in hand, while she ran around, too excited to stay in one place long, examining actual thriving, healthy plants, taking fertile soil samples, and living the dream that no Earth botanist in over a hundred of years had ever thought would be possible again. Of course, she'd gained his attention when she stripped off her clothes and waded into the lake. It had been a lovely way to end an extraordinary day.

Since then, they'd returned to the Oasis five more times. Each exploration as wonderful as the last. She never wanted this time to end.

But it had to—and soon.

Her skin grew cold, her smile disappearing. Despite her best efforts, she still hadn't had any brilliant insights into how to convince Command Council to allow a condemned criminal on that rescue shuttle. Detailing Caine's heroism and the way he'd saved Winthrop's life might earn him a few less years or some better rations, but she knew Caine was right. It might not even get him that. And it definitely wouldn't gain him a pardon. She needed more.

"If you want to have time to explore the outer rim of the Oasis, we should get going." His tone, once again alert, cut into her thoughts. Like her, he'd been ignoring the fact that their time together was reaching its end. At least when it came to making plans for her to return to her crew's camp.

On the other hand, he'd been fucking her like he intended to make up for a lifetime of missed opportunities.

She wasn't complaining. She felt equally as desperate for his touch.

She only wished he'd kissed her on the mouth just one of those times. But apparently, that was a line he was unwilling to cross. And, truly, she understood. Already, she could barely comprehend how she was going to leave him behind if she couldn't come up with a solution, even knowing what it would cost her family and everyone back on Earth.

"We need to be back at the cave before dusk," he reminded, though he made no move to get up.

"Agreed." Thanks to its two suns, a Dragath25 day was five hours longer than an Earth day, but the night was far shorter, lasting only three hours. Unfortunately, nocturnal predators on the planet made up for the short hunting time with their ferocity, amassing six or seven kills a night before slinking back to their underground lairs. She'd heard enough horrific shrieks and clawing sounds from the safety of Caine's cave to know she wanted to be inside by the time dusk arrived. "Just give me two more minutes to recover and we'll get started."

"We can always come back tomorrow." He squeezed her hand. She squeezed back.

She knew what he was doing. Ignoring the inevitable. Still...another day with Caine alone?

Joy rippled through her. Followed by a wave of guilt. She had no right to take such a risk when she needed to be near Winthrop when the rescue shuttle arrived. No right either to be so content while her brother and sister were in such a precarious position, while the survival of the approaching rescue crew was still in question, while Ava and Winthrop continued to struggle with Pogue at the scientist campsite.

But she couldn't help it. Couldn't help wanting just one more day together. Just the two of them.

And it wasn't as if they were shirking their main responsibilities.

They spent the majority of their day working on the jammer. It wasn't functional yet, but what Caine had managed to do already was nothing short of miraculous. Only when a break was needed did they train or visit the Oasis or, her personal favorite, make love. They separated only long enough for him to check on Ava.

Was it so wrong then to take one more day while she still could? Truly, she'd never felt so comfortable or content with another living soul in her life. The freedom and joy she'd found living with him was something she could never have imagined.

Sure, there were still issues she would have pushed if things had been less uncertain. Still times Caine's gaze grew shadowed, his mood distant. When the wonder and the need vanished from his stare and he felt a million metrals away. Plus, he hadn't mentioned the name Gwen again. Nor revealed anything about the actions that had branded him a criminal and landed him on Dragath25.

But he had told her other things. Like the fact that he'd graduated from the Academy and served as a pilot and a soldier—which had not surprised her at all. Or the fact that his parents had died when he was a baby and he'd lived on one of the last remaining farms with his uncle and aunt until blight destroyed that, too.

Like her, he'd lost a lot in his life.

Which was only one of a thousand reasons she wasn't leaving him behind when they got that jammer working. No matter what he'd done before. No matter what he said about being unable to go back to Earth. He deserved the same second chance he'd given her.

She just didn't know yet how she was going to do it—or how to convince him to trust she would.

"Okay, sleepy head. That's way more than two minutes." Caine's hand clamped around her wrist, and suddenly, she was upright, swaying on two legs.

More surprised than outraged, she jerked her wrist from his grasp. "Stop manhandling me."

"Funny, you weren't complaining a few minutes ago."

How could she be mad when he was making actual jokes? More and more each day. Plus, his assertion was true. "You're right." She stepped close, running her palms up each sculpted muscle. "I love the way you take charge when we're fucking."

His nostrils flared. She ducked before he could grab her close. Funny, but he really liked hearing that word on her lips. And she wasn't above using it to her advantage when the mood struck. "Oh, no, you don't," she teased. "I'm under strict orders to get to work."

He shook his head, but his eyes held no anger, only heat. "I didn't realize you were so obedient."

"I'm not."

He stalked toward her. "We'll see about that."

Two hours and three amazing orgasms later, she was feeling downright docile as she finally got to work. Another hour later, she'd measured at least six more of the unfamiliar species of trees and flora and collected a couple of promising seed and soil samples to add to the assortment now sprouting in makeshift pots outside Caine's cave. In the meantime, never more than a few steps behind, his spear in hand, Caine had managed to catch two Elkins, tiny creatures that bore a small resemblance to the rabbits that had once been equally abundant on Earth.

She wished the day never had to end.

Then something shiny off to the side caught her eye. Curious, she scurried over, dropping to her knees to sift through the soil. "Look at this."

He peered over her shoulder. "I've seen plenty of them in the dirt, but never as big or intact as that one. What is it?"

"Some kind of mineral." She ran her finger along the jagged edge. Shaped like large arrowhead, the piece was long and thin, but most interesting of all was the way it glimmered in the sun like a mirror. "I'm not sure, but it may be help explain why this soil, which seems like it would be so inhospitable to plant life, is able to sustain it. Unlike the rest of the soil, it's cool to the touch, indicating it's reflecting rather than absorbing the sun's rays." She slipped the precious piece into her pocket. "I'll see if I can find more."

"You've got three minutes. Then we need to head back."

"Yes, sir." She turned to find his mouth inches from her own. So close that, if she leaned back only a little, they'd be kissing.

He stood abruptly.

She tried not to care.

"I think I see another over there." He pointed to something shiny in the dirt a few paces away, his tone deliberately offhand.

"Great." She squeezed out a limp smile and told herself what they had was enough. That it was better if some lines weren't crossed.

They worked in silence for a few more minutes.

She was almost grateful when the distant roar of a tigos echoed off the cliffs.

"Doesn't sound too close." She scratched at the dirt, extracting another interesting seed in her palms. She'd always been able to lose herself in work.

"Still, it's nothing to ignore. Let's go."

"One more moment." She scurried forward to collect another sample.

Only to be thwarted by Caine's large boot in her path. "No. Now."

She would have protested, but one look at his serious expression had her nodding instead. "Now is good."

He didn't smile.

"Stay on the path." It was the first time he'd barked orders at her in days.

Marching single-file, she hurried to comply, only noticing now that the two suns were much lower in the sky than they'd been last time they started home from the Oasis.

Still, they made it out of the Oasis and onto to the narrow path that led to Caine's home without incident.

She was already dreaming of a good meal and coaxing a few more smiles from Caine when a sudden hiss halted her in place.

"Did you hear that?" she whispered.

Caine's spear was already out and poised to hurl. "Get behind me."

Knowing it was futile to argue, she pressed against the rock and squeezed by him. His arm closed around her back, pulling her close. "Move when I move. And get ready to run if I tell you to."

She nodded, her chin butting into his back.

It was times like these she wondered why they ever left the house. But without food, they'd starve. And she couldn't stay huddled inside for the rest of her life. If Dragath25 was her future, she had to face it head on.

Slow and steady, they moved as one up the twisted path.

"Shit." Caine's muttered curse had her peeking around his shoulder.

"What is that?" Fear made her voice shriller than intended. A giant rust-colored, snake-like creature as thick as three wide tree trunks blocked the path to their home. Sharp, spiky teeth protruded from its long snout as it prodded at something beneath one of the rocks, its tail twitching back and forth.

"It's a pythile."

Seemed like there might be more he needed to say. "Is it dangerous?"

"Yes. They move fast. Faster than we can run. And those teeth are not for show, though their usual method is to wrap round their food and squeeze it to death before tearing it apart."

Maybe he'd been right to try and only offer its name. "Let's head back down the path." She kept her voice low. "It hasn't noticed us yet."

"Thanks to the wind. It's kicking up and, thankfully, sending our scent downwind." He started backwards, his gaze locked on the creature. "We'll wait in a nearby cave on the ridge. We can ride out the night there if we have to. Won't be luxurious, but we'll live."

She was all for that.

They'd backtracked several metrals when a low snarl at her back raised goose bumps on her arms. Behind her, less than a shuttle's length away, was a tigos. Worse, unlike the snake-like creature, this predator's gaze was locked on her.

CHAPTER SEVENTEEN

Caine's low curse snapped Bella into action.

"Go," she pushed him toward home.

He snatched her arm, pulling him with her. "Stay close." He was sprinting so fast her boots barely touched the ground. Another snarl sounded even closer, as loud as thunder.

"Don't look back," he shouted. "When I tell you to drop, do it."

"What are you going to do?"

But he was already swiveling around. "Drop!" He pushed her down, bounding over her, spear raised.

Her heart slammed into her throat.

It had been terrifying the first time he'd taken on a tigos. Now that she cared for him, it was excruciating.

She held her breath, her feet frozen to the ground, her hands outstretched as if she could hold him to her. The space was so narrow there was no way he could use the same killing technique he'd employed before. And still, man and beast ran at each other head on.

She opened her mouth to cry out his name—and then snapped it shut. He couldn't afford the distraction. His name emerged as a whispered plea instead. Her hands dropped to her side.

In the next instant, Caine stunned her by running up the side of the cliff in a gravity-defying acrobatic move that she would have sworn was next to impossible. He hovered for a second above the creature. Then, before gravity could win, launched himself forward—her cry strangling in her throat—before flipping in midair to land on the animal's back, his legs locking around its thick neck.

On instinct, her eyes slammed shut. Then she forced them wide, not wanting to take her eyes off him for an instant. As if the force of her stare alone could keep him safe.

The creature reared back, trying to shake him off.

With a roar, Caine drove his spear into its neck, but the hide was tougher than its belly. Blood trickled from the wound, but it didn't go down. Enraged, the creature swung its head, raking its fang down Caine's leg.

Nausea burned the back of her throat. Streaks of crimson appeared all too vivid against Caine's flesh.

"No." Shaking off her stupor, she ran toward them, the gourd clutched in her hand. It wasn't much, but if she aimed it just right, it might buy Caine a few critical seconds.

"Stay back," he shouted, burying his spear in the tigos' thick neck a second time.

She wouldn't have listened, but another sound—one that couldn't be ignored—had her swiveling around.

From the other direction, closing in fast, was the pythile, drawn by the scent of blood. Its body so wide it rubbed against both sides of the canyon path, its eyes glittering with hunger as it locked on the bleeding man and creature.

Her mouth went dry.

Caine was in trouble. Her, too.

Everything seemed to slow. The hammer of her heart against her ribs. The shallow rasp of her breath. Even the undulating slither of the pythile as it thundered toward her.

She knew what she had to do.

Leaping frantically at the canyon wall, she searched for a handhold. A crack. Anything she could use to heave herself up. Her nails ripped. Sharp points tore at the pads of her fingers. But thanks to Caine's training, she'd grown tougher. Stronger. Her shoulder still might burn, the old ache from the crash suddenly coming back to haunt her, but it wasn't enough to stop her. She kept searching.

Almost screaming with relief when her fingers found a crevice and she pulled herself upward. Her feet pedaled furiously against the rock wall as she reached for another handhold. And another. And another. Refusing to look down, refusing to contemplate failure.

Until the snake-like beast streaked passed, a rush of wind against her calves, not even giving her perch a second look. *Success!*

The second it was past, she let go. Exactly as planned.

Only instead of landing gracefully on her feet, she scraped along the wall as she went down, each sharp rock taking its pound of flesh, crash landing on one foot while the other buckled. An agonizing pain shot through her ankle.

"No! What are you doing?" roared Caine. "Get back up there."

She really wished he'd worry for himself.

Hopping on her one good leg, she dug for the gourd in her pocket, took a deep breath to steady herself, and hurled it as hard as she could at the pythile's retreating form.

The gourd pinged against the creature's hide. But there was no sound. No gash. Not even a damn scrape. *Turn, you bastard, turn!*

As if hearing her prayers, the animal swung its head around. Its nostrils twitching, keen to determine if what had happened signaled a threat.

Wasting no time, she pulled the reflective arrowhead from her pocket. She only had seconds before the pythile lost interest and continued following the scent of blood straight to Caine.

Hands shaking, she tilted the mineral this way and that, muttering to herself until—thankfully—it worked. The sun glinted off the mineral, shining right into the creature's slitted eyes.

It hissed and shook its head, a forked tongue the length of a human leg flickering out.

"That's right, big guy." Voice trembling, she shook the mineral back and forth as she limped backward up the trail. "Don't you want to follow me? Don't you want to know what this is?"

Hissing, flicking its tongue, the pythile rippled after her. Its narrow red eyes blinked rapidly as it tried to dodge the light.

Below her on the path, she could hear Caine shouting, but she couldn't hear what. She had every confidence, though, that with the pythile out of his way, he'd be able to finish off the tigos in no time flat. In fact, she was counting on it.

She'd gone a good twenty steps when she realized her distraction tactic was coming to an end.

The hair at the back of her neck prickled. The pythile was growing bored. Or maybe it had simply adjusted to the light. Whatever the case, its pupils, which had been big and wide at the start, had narrowed to pinpricks, making its eyes an even creepier red. At the same time, its tail twitched faster and faster.

She didn't have to be a pythile expert to conclude it was shifting back into hunt mode.

With a shout, she took off running, her ankle protesting with every frantic stride. Sweat dripped down the curve of her back. Stung her eyes. Still, she didn't stop. And she didn't look back.

The cave was a shining beacon of hope less than fifty paces away.

Caine had another spear placed right inside the door. If she could get it, there was a chance she could stab the beast and help Caine. Or she would die fighting.

Either way, she wanted the chance to try.

The ground shook beneath her boots, proof the pythile was closing the gap.

And then it was so close its warm breath blasted against her back. So close its wild, feral stench flooded her lungs.

Her hands curled into fists. Her eyes sank closed. She wasn't going to make it. All her plans....Caine....Her throat grew tight.

Then suddenly, the pythile shrieked.

Bella flinched, her head swiveling around. In the settling dust, Caine loomed right behind, his expression fierce as he struck the pythile's tail over and over while the creature writhed in pain.

"Go," he urged. "Get inside. Barricade the door."

On autopilot, she scrambled forward. Her side screaming at her, her ankle a constant pain. It seemed to take a million hours to cover the last leg to the cave.

Then, thankfully, she was wrenching open the door, her gaze searching frantically in the dark for the spear.

Her hand closed over smooth wood. Relief slammed through her. *Just hold on one more minute, Caine.*

She turned to run outside.

Only to crash into an immoveable object.

Caine. He stood in the doorway, his chest heaving, his beautiful body covered in scratches and blood. But he was alive.

Her spear clattered to the ground.

"Thank God. You did it. You saved us both." She stared up at him, too exhausted to move, too relieved to do anything but shoot him a crazy, wide grin. "Though you have to admit that use of the arrowhead was pretty ingenious for such short notice." Just beyond his wide shoulder, outlined in the open door, she could see the pythile lying still in the dirt. "For a moment there, I really thought those bastards were going to get us. I—"

"Where did you think you were going with that?" He cut her off, his voice hard, his gaze locked on the spear at her feet.

Alarm whispered through her. Something wasn't right. Caine wasn't...right. His gaze was even harder than the first time she'd laid eyes on him.

She backed up a few steps, her ankle throbbing. "I was coming to help."

"I told you to stay inside." A muscle ticked in his jaw. "Just like I told you to stay on that cliff. Just like I told you to drop that damn arrowhead and make a run for it."

"And leave you to fight them alone? Not likely."

His nostrils flared. "So you thought you'd die instead?"

"I was hoping it would be neither of us."

That only seemed to make him madder. "Hoping? Hope doesn't get you anything but dead on this fucking planet." He slammed the door closed. She got the distinct impression he wasn't so much shutting everything else out as locking her in.

She took a few more steps back. "But that didn't happen." She spoke in the same coaxing tone she'd used with the pythile. "I'm okay. You're okay. We both survived."

"It's not okay." He started toward her, his hands fisting by his side. For the first time since he'd told her his name, she felt wary around the man who'd become her protector. "I'm supposed to keep you safe. I'm supposed to keep you alive....You want to know who Gwen was?"

Dread washed over Bella. She nodded anyway.

"She was my wife." Pain twisted his features into a mask of anguish. "And I couldn't keep her alive. She was stubborn and stupid and she didn't listen to me, and she died. Murdered by a corrupt bastard because she refused to heed my warnings. Now she's nothing but dirt while I pay penance in a hell that doesn't even require an afterlife."

"I'm so sorry." Bella's voice was little more than a whisper.

It was as if he didn't hear her. As if old demons had taken hold and drowned out anything else.

"I'm not going to let the same thing happen with you." He jerked a strap used for tanning meat from the table, wrapping it around one fist before pulling it taut. "I thought we settled this last time, but I guess not. I guess you need to have it driven home. I guess I've been too soft and let things go too far. While you're here with me, you're going to obey me. You're going to get it through your pretty, stubborn head that this is a dictatorship. That I rule and you follow." The strap cracked ominously in his hands. "You may hate me when we're through, but if that's what it takes to keep you alive, so be it."

"No." She backpedaled faster, bumping into a stool before righting herself. "You're not thinking clearly. Whatever you're planning on doing with that won't solve anything."

He kicked the stool out of his way. "It will keep you safe."

She sprinted for the door. He caught her easily, his arm a tight band around her waist as he carried her kicking and screaming to the bed.

She landed in the middle in a tangle of limbs. She tried to use one of his fighting moves, but he subdued her easily, flipping her onto her stomach, grabbing hold of her wrists with one hand. The rough edge of the blanket pressed into her cheek. His knee a heavy weight against her spine, not hurting her, but holding her down just the same.

"I'll never forgive you."

"At least you'll be alive." He jerked her pants down her hips, leaving her ass bare. Her skin prickled.

She turned her face away, bracing for the pain. "I never knew you were a coward, but I'm glad to learn it now."

He stilled above her. "I'm no coward."

"You don't think I don't see what you're doing?" She tugged against his grip. No give. "Five amazing days together, and now, when you think the end is near, you're back to pushing me away so you don't have to feel anything at all. So you don't have to risk caring for anyone else that might leave you or die." She bit back a sob. "It's almost as if you're begging me to hate you so things can go back to the way they were."

"You don't know what you're talking about." But his hold weakened.

She seized the opportunity, bucking him off her back and spinning over. He loomed above, his sweat-slicked chest heaving, his gaze heavy with uncertainty, the strap dangling useless in one fist.

"You want me to hate you. You want me to leave you here." She stared up at him. "All this time, you wouldn't consider even the possibility of a way to convince Command Council to commute your sentence and get you off this hellhole and I thought...I thought maybe it was because you weren't sure about me. Weren't sure you trusted me to stand up for you as you've done for me. But now I see that was all wrong. The problem isn't me. And it isn't Dragath25. It's you. You're afraid. Afraid to care too deeply or hope too intensely for better than this miserable existence." She fumbled with her clothes. "I don't know what happened with your wife, but I'd rather die a thousand times over than spend whatever time I have left with someone who's too afraid to take a chance and really live."

He closed his eyes, his whole body folding in on itself as he sat back on his heels.

She was too angry to care.

She kicked out, hitting him square in the chest. He toppled over the side of the bed.

Seizing the advantage as he'd taught her, she leapt off the bed and stood over him. She knew he wouldn't come after her again. That he'd never really physically hurt her. It wasn't in his nature. But pushing her away—well, that apparently was in his blood.

"The Council might have marooned you on Dragath25, but you're the one making the sentence lonely and miserable. Look at this place." She flung her hands outward. "It's like a jail cell. And the only time you let yourself feel good is during sex. You're punishing yourself for no good reason."

He snarled up at her. "You've been on this damn planet for less than two weeks. You think you have the right to judge? Dragath25 is one of the most dangerous places in the universe. You have to stay on guard all the time or you'll be dead."

"What an excellent justification. But staying on guard against outside elements isn't the same as guarding yourself against any kind of joy or happiness. Against another person."

He bristled, jumping to his feet, forcing her to stumble back. "I'm not sure what you're complaining about. Our deal was protection for pleasure. I'm fulfilling that and then some."

"You're right." A wave of pain swept through her. "You promised me nothing else. And you've given me all you agreed to and more." She took a step back. And then another. "I'll always be grateful for how you saved me and my colleagues. I'll always be grateful for your patience and your kindness when you could have used force and taken without giving anything in return. But I won't stay with you if fear is all you can offer."

His hands fisted by his side. "You're making a mistake. It's too dangerous for you out there without me."

"Maybe so, but it's a risk I'm willing to take. We could have forged something great here on Dragath25, but you won't let that happen." Her hand closed over the door latch. She looked back, taking one last look at the room where she'd been surprisingly happy these last few days. "Looks like I lied about the anything part, huh?"

His haunted gaze met hers.

"Good-bye, Caine. Be safe. I truly wish you only the best. You may not believe it but, Dragath25 criminal or not, you deserve it."

CHAPTER EIGHTEEN

"I like you bent over like that, Cadet West. Gives a man ideas."

Ignoring Pogue's crude comments, Bella slid her hands a little farther under the heavy boulder and heaved. No luck. It didn't budge. After almost a week, her sprained ankle was pretty much healed, but that didn't mean she could lift such a huge rock by herself.

She swallowed her pride. "Any chance you can grab the other side of this rock? I need to stack it with the others."

"No way." Pogue's gaze lifted to the sky. "I'm not doing a damn thing to discourage the rescue team's arrival."

"Even if it means their deaths?" She'd told him a hundred times about Caine's explanation for what had happened to their ship and what might happen to the next that tried to land.

"Just because you're willing to believe the ravings of a prisoner stuck too long on this planet doesn't mean I have to."

He'd been against her idea from the start. Only Winthrop's backing had saved her project from being dismantled while she watched.

Maybe Pogue was right. But she didn't think so. Which was why, despite Pogue's displeasure, she was so intent on using the rocks to spell out a warning. Sure, it was ridiculously low tech, but at least it was something—and something was better than doing nothing.

"Will you at least help me improve our camp's defenses?" She kept hoping she would find a way to lessen tensions between her and Pogue. "I'd like to use the leftover rocks to narrow the cave entrance." She wanted to be prepared for anything—especially a future on Dragath25. Bleak as it now seemed without Caine in her life.

She rubbed at her chest. Darn thing wouldn't stop aching. Maybe Caine had been right all along. Maybe Dragath25 wasn't the kind of place that brought anything but pain.

Not that she was simply going to curl up and wait to die.

She carried a spear with her everywhere she went. It might not have been as strong or well-made as Caine's, but it would get the job done against beast or man. She'd even managed to catch one scrawny Elkin, though that had probably been more luck than skill.

She was still waiting on Pogue's answer when a shadow fell over her. Her heart gave a tiny leap before she could stop it. Stupid thing was always doing that even though it had been a week now and still no Caine. That particular organ didn't seem able to accept it wouldn't be seeing him again.

But out of sight didn't mean out of mind. She still intended to do everything in her power to have his sentence absolved if she and her crew were, by some miracle, actually rescued. No matter how things had ended between them, Caine was a good man. He didn't deserve to die on Dragath25. Protecting him had become as essential to her as safeguarding her siblings and all the others depending on her and this mission to save them from famine and death. Fortunately, the seeds of a plan had finally started to germinate.

Shading her eyes against the sun, she looked back at the source of the shadow and forced a smile. "Hello, Dr.

Winthrop. How are you feeling?" Things between them had been decidedly awkward since her return.

"Better, thanks." He patted his chest, his movements stiff. "The bandages are definitely working and the ribs holding." His smile was tentative. "Thanks to you, I'll be back to one hundred percent very soon."

"But not today," taunted Pogue. He stepped forward, forcing Winthrop back. Tension between the two officers was worse than ever. "Now, where did you want this, Bella?" The reason for his sudden pretense of cooperation obvious, he flexed his bare chest as he picked up the rock she'd thought would require two people. "The Doctor here may not be able to get the job done, but I can. Fact is, I can go as long as you need."

Unfortunately for her, Pogue seemed to have an unending supply of annoying innuendos.

She honestly wasn't sure how best to handle the man. She needed him and his guns, but it felt like a devil's bargain. One that was slowly unraveling. His smirk when she'd first returned had been irritating, but the way he'd been looking at her since made her skin crawl. Like she was his for the taking. And he followed her everywhere she went. Made crude comments and promises whenever he could. She feared it wouldn't be long before the last of the Council influence disintegrated and he moved from innuendos to action.

Another reason she always had her spear at hand.

She'd wanted to steal a gun and strike out separately with Winthrop and Ava, but they'd adamantly refused. Winthrop, with typical Council arrogance, had assured her he could handle Pogue. While Ava was obsessed with the soil on the nearby ridge—and growing more edgy with every day closer to the rescue shuttle's scheduled arrival. She'd become convinced that solving the mysteries of Dragath25 soil held the key to not only saving Earth, but herself.

So, unless they changed their minds, Bella was stuck with Pogue. She wasn't leaving Winthrop and Ava again.

"Please bring the rock to the cave entrance." Choosing to capitalize on Pogue's short-term willingness to cooperate, she picked up a smaller rock and crab-walked it over to the cave to show him the exact location. "I want to shrink the opening so that only one person can enter at a time. It will make it too small for tigos to get through and give us the chance to pick off any unwelcome human visitors one by one."

"Blood-thirsty." Pogue dropped his rock and crowded in far too close. "I knew you were more than a great piece of ass."

"Get back." Annoyed, she jammed her elbow into his side.

He didn't even grunt. "Why?" His voice was an ugly growl. "You only do lowlife convicts?"

"Officer Pogue," Winthrop appeared behind them, his expression full of righteous fury, "we may not be aboard a Council shuttle, but protocol still applies. Watch yourself or the Council will be hearing about more than your initial indiscretion."

Pogue's face turned bright, angry red. "I'd watch yourself, too, Doc. This planet can be a dangerous place." Then, with his threat hanging in the air, he stalked off.

Bella watched him go, her unease growing.

"Sorry," Winthrop's apologetic stare was fixed on the unfinished tower of rocks. "I didn't mean to run him off when you needed help."

"No, I'm grateful. He's more aggressive every day."

Winthrop ran a hand through his hair, his usual short Academy haircut having been replaced by a long, shaggy look that made him appear all the more boyish. "Damn planet is turning everyone into someone else. Savages, criminals; it's impossible to know who anyone is any more. And he probably thinks because you were willing to fuck that convict, you'll fuck anything." He flinched. "Not that I meant you...."

"No, it's good to stop dancing around it." She took a deep breath. She would never be so blunt if they were still on Earth, but things had changed. *She* had changed. "I'm sorry you were disappointed by some of my recent choices, but I did what I thought was best for me, my brother and sister, and you. I don't regret it. Not for a second." She met his gaze straight on. "Caine isn't just some convict. He's a good man."

"So why didn't you stay with him if he's so great?" Winthrop's voice was tinged with anger.

"I wanted more than he could give." It was weird to say it aloud. She hadn't even discussed it with Ava. It had felt too painful. "Everyone is always saying Dragath25 is so different, but when it comes to people, we're the same any planet over. Same needs. Same stupid fights. Same ability to get mad and wound each other."

Apparently, the more you cared about someone, the more furious you were when they disappointed you—and the more stupid you behaved in the aftermath.

"I never had much luck at relationships back on Earth," she admitted. "I guess I should have realized going to a different part of the universe wouldn't change that. But that doesn't mean Caine doesn't deserve our help. He saved our lives. He should be allowed his as well. "

Winthrop's hand gripped hers. "What a mess." Red shaded the tips of his ears. "I thought we'd come here, find the answers we needed to save Earth, and together, you and I would find fame and glory and...more." His blush grew deeper. "It was a foolish fantasy for an officer who's been wrapped up in his work too long."

This time her smile was real. "It's not a foolish fantasy. You deserve all that and more." She squeezed his hand. "You just need to find the right girl."

His expression sobered. "And get the hell off of Dragath25."

She let out a long sigh. "If that's even possible." Her gaze shifted to her pile of rocks before finding his. "Did you know before we left that other ships had been brought down? That this mission might not be the simple in and out you said?"

He kicked the dirt with his boot. "The Council informed me there'd been trouble with a few past ships, but the cause of the crashes weren't known. There was no reason to believe it wasn't pilot error. Or simple bad luck. Certainly none clear cut enough reason to keep us from our humanitarian mission." His eyes were clear of deception and begged her to understand. "I would never have put you in danger if I'd thought there was really a chance we'd crash, too."

"Thank you." It would have to be enough. She and Winthrop would never again have the clear-cut, protocol-sanctioned relationship that had guided their interactions before the crash, but they were on their way to building something more real.

"Try not to worry too much," he urged. "The rescue team will definitely be more cautious in their approach. Dismissing this latest crash as pilot error won't be so easy yet again."

"How do we know they'll come at all? Maybe they'll decide it's too dangerous."

"They'll come. They know there is at least one Command Council survivor." The tips of his ears turned red again. "It's why we put the tracker in me as opposed to the ship. To contend with precisely this kind of scenario. Not to mention that the Command Council is desperate to know what we've found. It's why they insisted I keep mum about the potential dangers of this mission in the first place. I shouldn't discuss Command Council business, but they need this mission to succeed." His voice dropped. "They're nervous. Too much more failure and famine and they'll lose the hold they have on the people."

Such a tangled web.

She could only imagine how complicated it would become if the Command Council learned replicating the same conditions on Earth as Dragath25 would be impossible without extensive water supplies. Not only would the race be on to civilize and then strip Dragath25 of all its plants and soil, but all its water as well. The Council would stop at nothing to protect their power and add to their coffers. A scenario she didn't think 225 and his pack would easily allow. And Caine would be right in the middle of it all.

She swallowed hard. At least now, thanks to Winthrop's revelations, she knew what she had to do.

Winthrop's gaze shifted to the sky. "By my calculations, they'll be here any day now." His expression brightened. "We'll be able to go home."

"Not if the shuttle crashes."

Winthrop was as bad as all the rest on this point. Despite knowing about the previous crashes, he seemed almost deliberate in his refusal to consider what would likely happen to the rescue shuttle when it tried to find them. She'd witnessed it before with him. He preferred to bury his head in the sand when the predicted outcome didn't suit what he wanted.

But she couldn't let him get away with it this time. After all, she couldn't save anyone, least of all Caine and her siblings, if she couldn't stop the rescue shuttle from crashing.

"We have to figure out how to warn them. We can't just hope for the best. Or think my pathetic pile of rocks spelling out danger will be enough of a warning." She didn't think Caine would stop working on his jammer, but she couldn't know for sure—and even he hadn't been certain he could ever get it to work in the first place. "Let's meet in an hour to brainstorm more ideas. But first I'm going to bring some more rocks for defense. You should have Ava check on your bandage. And tell her we've made up. She worries about us all."

She turned to go. His hand landed on her shoulder. "I don't want you to think what happened before...with that prisoner...matters. Once we get off this hellhole, everything here will seem like a bad dream. Easily forgotten."

Her stomach turned over. She knew he meant his words as a kindness, but what if she didn't want to forget? Caine was a memory she intended to hold onto forever. And she was never going back to the accepting lump she'd been under Command Council protocol. She understood why Winthrop clung to the system. It served him well. But she wanted better for her brother and sister. For herself.

"Pogue, come quick!" The panicked shout of one of the soldiers drew her attention. Within seconds, she was hurrying to where the soldiers had gathered. Winthrop right behind.

"What's wrong?" Her words came out in a wheezing rush.

Pogue looked worried. "Ransom says he can't find Pratt or Cadet Davies."

"What?" She grabbed Ransom's arm. A short squat guy with a permanent blank stare, he was content to take orders and ask no question, the perfect underling for Pogue. "Where did you last see them?"

"On the plateau." Ransom pointed up and to the left. "I was on watch."

It was the small plateau they'd all climbed numerous times. Ava had been particularly keen on collecting soil samples from there these last couple of days. Dirt was her specialty, and she'd agreed that those reflective mineral arrowheads might just be the most critical discovery of this mission. Though Bella had noticed her colleague had also taken to just going up there to stare at the sky, a haunted look on her face.

"Cadet Davies was working," continued Ransom, "and Pratt was supposed to relieve me for lookout duty. I saw them coming down the cliff, near the caves. Then something bright flashed overhead and…and I must have blinked. When I looked down, they were gone."

"Shit." Mitchell, Pogue's second-in-command and a first-grade asshole in his own right, shifted restlessly, his usual smirk nowhere to be seen. "I hate this place."

"One of them must have fallen. Or been hurt." Bella tugged on Ransom's arm. "Show me where you last saw them. We need to find them before something else does."

Ransom shook his head, his boots locked into the dirt, his gaze on Pogue. "I looked for them on the way down." He swallowed hard. "All I found was Pratt's gun."

"That can't be."

Ransom's frown lengthened. "I'm telling you. I looked. I shouted. They weren't there. Just Pratt's gun. No signs of even a scuffle. Or footprints. It's like they just disappeared."

"They've got to be somewhere," Bella snapped. "We have to widen our search."

Pogue swung his gun from his shoulder, positioning it in front of him at the ready. His gaze scanned the perimeter. "We need to get to our own cave."

Without hesitation, Ransom fell into line beside him. The five remaining soldiers did the same.

"No." Bella could not believe Pogue was doing this again. "We can't cower inside. We need to go look for them."

"And die with them?" sneered Mitchell.

Pogue's hard gaze bore into her. "I've already lost too many men. I'm not losing any more." His stare flickered to Winthrop, challenge in his gaze. "I'm certain the Command Council would agree as that's standard crisis protocol." He gave the signal to move out. "Keep your guns at the ready, men. We don't know what's out there." Dust filled the air as the soldiers' boots shuffled forward.

A hand grabbed her arm. "I'll go with you to look. Council protocol or not." Winthrop stood by her side, a determined look on his face. "We're not leaving Ava out there."

Relief washed over Bella, but it was short-lived. A quick scan of Winthrop proved he was breathing heavily from even that short run. Even more telling, the hand wrapped around his rib revealed the true extent of his pain. He'd never be able to help her against whatever was out there.

There was only one man who could.

"Jim, thank you." She covered his hand with hers, hiding her small smile at the way his eyes widened in surprise at her brazen use of his first name. "But you need to stay here." She searched for an explanation that would leave him some pride. "We have no idea what condition Ava and Pratt will be in when I bring them back." She refused to contemplate any other alternative. "I need you to be ready with supplies by the time I return. We know Pogue won't have done a damn thing."

"That's crazy. You can't go alone."

She squeezed his hand. "I…I won't be alone."

Understanding dawned, pain and resentment flaring in Winthrop's eyes before his expression shuddered altogether. "I see."

She didn't have time to gently handle a Command Council ego right now.

"Caine is Ava's best hope." At least she hoped he would be. After the terrible way they'd parted, she didn't know if he would help her or not. But she'd beg. She'd grovel. She'd do anything if it meant finding Ava.

Spear locked tight in her grip, she took off at a run.

She'd gone about half a metral when a large object stepped into her path.

CHAPTER NINETEEN

Bella opened her mouth to scream, her spear coming up and forward.

"It's me." Caine blocked her thrust with his arm.

"*Oh, my God*, I'm sorry. I saw a dark blur. I thought you were something else." Her gaze ran the length of him. His scratches had healed. He looked good. And strong. And close enough to touch. Her chest grew tight. "Did I hurt you?"

He shook his head, his expression grim. "You thought I was whatever got Ava."

Surprise thundered through her. "You know?"

"I heard."

"How?"

A beat of silence. "I was watching."

"Watching?" She didn't understand. "Did you see what took them?"

Regret flickered across his face. "I wasn't watching Ava." His stare bore into her.

Because he was watching me.

A warm feeling swept through her. All this time, she'd thought he'd let her go without a fight, but he'd been with her all along. Still protecting her. Still guarding her. Despite all that had happened.

There was so much to say, but only one thing she could ask right now. "Will you help me find her?"

"Of course."

That was all it took.

They spent the next several hours looking. They started at the last known sighting and worked outward in larger and larger circles, searching the caves and the surrounding area.

In the end, they found nothing. Which meant there was truly nothing to find. No footprints. No signs of struggle. No clues as to what had happened to Ava or the other soldier Pratt. Because Caine's tracking skills were amazing and meticulous, and if there had been anything to find, he would have.

By the time evening came, despair and desperation had settled over her like a heavy cloak. Thoughts of her friend hurt or afraid played over and over in her mind until she thought she might grow mad.

"Bella, look out."

Caine's sharp warning brought her head jerking up. She took a hurried shuffle-step to the side. She'd been so focused on scouring the ground right in front of her that she hadn't realized she'd ventured too close to the cliff edge.

"I think you need to stop." His black gaze flickered in the light of the glow stick he pulled from his pack.

"No. I'm not stopping. You…you should go. I know it's only going to get more dangerous as the night wears on, and I don't want you running into Pogue and his men either. I can't thank you enough for all you've done."

He stared at her, his jaw tight, frustration pouring off him—and she braced herself for another scene like at his home—but he didn't say another word. Didn't bark an order. Or stalk toward her. Instead, after one more disapproving look in her direction, he turned and resumed searching again.

If she hadn't been so terrified for Ava, she would have broken down with relief and gratitude. But now wasn't the time so she blinked hard against the sudden sting in her eyes and returned to the tedious task of examining the ground for any sign that might tell her what had happened to her friend.

Another two hours later the glow stick began to fade while the hisses and howls of tigos and Dragath25's nocturnal creatures grew louder and more frequent and the ground was literally starting to blur. So much so, she missed a big rock right in front of her face.

She stumbled and would have fallen flat if strong arms hadn't caught her.

"That's it." This time Caine's declaration brooked no argument. There was no anger in his voice, no wildness either, only determination. He set her solidly on her feet and dropped his arms.

She missed his warmth.

"We're done looking for tonight," he declared. "We both need to be alert and well if we have any shot of finding Ava."

He was right. She knew he was right and still…it was hard to give up. "I don't understand why we can't find any clue of what might have taken them or where they went."

"It's definitely strange." There was an unusual hesitance to his voice.

"Why does it sound like you known something you're not telling me?"

He shifted his weight from one boot to the other. "I've heard rumors. Rumors of other prisoners disappearing into thin air."

"Taken by something like the saybak?" The thought of Ava in the clutches of that flying beast made her sick.

"No, those creatures are vegetarians. They may use fire when threatened, but they don't go around stealing people from the sky." He worked his jaw as if he were debating whether to say more.

"Tell me, please."

"When I first arrived, there was talk that Earth wasn't the only one using this planet. Prisoners whispered not to get caught alone. Until today, I thought those rumors were just another scare tactic by 225 and his men to keep the others in line."

"Not the only ones? Are you...do you mean...aliens?"

A few centuries ago, scientists had figured out how to travel to adjacent solar systems—an amazing accomplishment celebrated for a short time as the hope of humanity's future—until it was discovered that no other habitable planets existed within. Plans to explore farther, to figure out how to travel greater distances had been in the development stages when the first waves of famine and blight had hit and efforts had to be abandoned. Still, speculation had been rife that further exploration would not only uncover more livable planets, but contact with alien life.

To think that it had happened already. On Dragath25. And that Ava had been taken by some of them....

"Oh, God," Bella whispered. "If it was aliens, we'll never find her."

Caine's hands fisted at his side. "I didn't say it was true. Just that it was something we need to consider. We'll know more after we search again tomorrow. I want to take another look at the caves in the light."

"Right." She stared at his hands. Wishing he would unclasp them and put his arms around her. Touch her. Hold her. Comfort her. But the fact was, she had no right to ask. That had never been their deal to begin with.

And she was far less certain of where they stood now than ever before.

Tension vibrated between them, a livewire of awareness she didn't know how to interpret. He'd set no terms for what he wanted in return for his help searching for Ava. She wasn't even sure what she wished he'd ask for, though the thought of saying goodbye and simply walking away made her eyes sting all over again.

"There's a small overhang less than five metrals from where Ava was taken," he said at last. "We'll stay there for the night."

So…she was staying with him.

Her relief was embarrassingly immense. As were her nerves. They'd never been lovers in the true sense of the word, and yet he knew her body, her dark needs and cravings, better than anyone. From the first time, his touch had brought her nothing but pleasure. He'd seen the best and worst of her. It made her feel close to him in a way she'd never felt for another living soul. And vulnerable. Too vulnerable.

She hadn't been wrong about any of the things she'd said to him after the tigos attack, but she wished now that she'd stopped to think if maybe things weren't so black and white. She'd accused him of being afraid, but the fact was, she'd been afraid, too. Afraid of being rejected. Afraid she was becoming nothing more than another burden. Afraid he cared too little. Afraid she'd never measure up to a wife she hadn't even known he'd had. So she'd run before giving him time to make things right.

But she wasn't running now. Because time away had let her see that, as much as it hurt to have only a small part of him, it hurt a lot worse to have none at all.

Determined, she stepped beneath the overhang. Soft, comforting light spilled into the space indicating Caine had engaged yet another of his glow sticks. A heavy hand fell on her shoulder.

"Bella?"

She swiveled around, her throat tight. She liked hearing her name on his lips.

"I'm sorry."

She stared at him, her heart beating hard. Was he expressing regret over Ava's disappearance? Or what had happened between them? His grim expression gave nothing away.

"Helping me look for Ava today," she began, "that's more than I can ever repay."

"I don't want repayment." The glow stick thudded to the ground. His hands cupped her shoulders, his voice rough and low. "I don't want anything in return." He cleared his throat. "I shouldn't have gone after you like that. I said you'd be safe with me, and then I did the unthinkable."

"You were dealing with some old stuff, I think." She wasn't going to tip-toe around the issue anymore. "Your wife and what happened with her."

"That's no excuse. I trained as a soldier and a pilot and spent a lot of years fighting on Earth. But I never once raised a hand against a woman. Even when Gwen and I weren't getting along. Even when she slept around. I don't think I deserve praise for that. It's…it's just how a real man behaves. But…but I lost it with you and," he blew out a breath, "and I've done a lot of bad shit in my life, but I never felt truly ashamed until that moment."

Needing to touch him, she slid her hands along his skin until her palms covered his wide shoulders. "Like you said, this place twists us all. You're a good man."

She could scarcely believe he was sharing so much of himself.

He swallowed hard. "By the time we met, I'd become more beast than man. Living alone. Caring only for myself. But you changed that. Touching you, being with you, watching you care so much for everyone and everything around you, brought me a little bit more back to myself. And the thought of losing that…of losing you…." His hold tightened. "You were one hundred percent right. I was afraid. I didn't want to let you in further. I didn't want to go back to what I was before you….then I lost you anyway."

"You haven't lost me." She pressed her body flush against his. The knowledge that he cared for her, that she was as important to him as he was to her, was more than she'd ever hoped to hear. "I'm right here."

He wrapped his arms around her. "I'm a lot more than a Dragath25 low life and a lot more than that bully chickenshit I became in that moment." He pressed his forehead against hers. "I want the chance to prove it to you."

"I already know." Her fingers tangled in the short hair at his nape.

"I finished the device." His fingers contracted against her skin. "There's no one hundred percent guarantee, but I think I can get that pile of wires to work well enough to jam 225's weapon and allow your rescue team to land safely." He cleared his throat. "You can go home, Bella."

"*Oh, my God,*" She jumped up and down, almost knocking the top of her head into his chin. She could scarcely believe it. Caine could save those people. No one else needed to die. Her sister and brother would continue to be safe, too. And once the rescue shuttle landed, they could join the search for Ava. Her friend would be found. All thanks to Caine. "You are amazing. Thank you so much."

His hold tightened. "It's no guarantee. Just remember that. There's a lot that could still go wrong."

"I understand.'" She tried to contain her sense of hope. "Nothing on Dragath25 is easy."

His thumb whispered across her lower lip. "Except touching you."

Her heart fluttered. "So touch me." Her nails scraped gently down his back. "I missed you."

She was lifted in the next instant, his hands sliding under her ass as he took control, his dark gaze holding her captive as he walked them backwards deeper under the overhang. "I missed you, too. Turns out holding back didn't do a damn thing to squelch the pain. I still saw you everywhere. Smelled you on our bed. Heard your voice on the wind. The cave, the ridge, the spring, the Oasis…it all felt damn lonely without you."

She pressed a kiss to his jaw. "So you came to watch over me. Thank you."

"I shadowed you from the instant you left." His hold tightened, his gaze darkened by a vulnerability that hadn't been there before. "I'd die to protect you, Bella."

"No one's dying." Her tone was fierce. "Thanks to you, we're both getting off this miserable planet."

He tensed further.

"Caine? You know we're both getting off this planet, right? Your device isn't just going to save the rest of us, but you, too." She cradled his jaw. "Even when I left your cave, I never intended to leave you behind. We're all going home."

He turned and kissed her palm. "I can't go back, Bella."

CHAPTER TWENTY

Caine slid her down his hard body as if already putting distance between them.

She grabbed his shoulders, keeping him close. "Don't give me that bullshit about being a killer and deserving punishment. I don't know what you did, but I know enough about you now to realize there was a good reason behind it."

"That means a lot." But the resignation was still there.

"Tell me," she urged, "tell me what happened."

She didn't need to hear his story to know he had a valid reason for what he'd done. She knew it by the man he was, but she could sense his need to tell.

She was also more than ready for him to let her in.

He blew out a breath. "It's not a pretty tale." He turned away. She felt cold without his big body to warm her. "My wife Gwen was a good person, but she didn't always make the best choices. About a year after we were married, she got involved with a married Councilman notorious for sleeping around. A guy named Hendricks."

Bella fought not to grimace. She's heard of Councilman Hendricks. While hardly beloved by the general populace, he'd managed to advance in the Council leadership and was considered the third most powerful man in the entire Earth government.

She suddenly understood Caine's pessimism. If Hendricks was the one who'd sent Caine here, they'd be going up against the whole Council to get him out.

"When I found out about Gwen and Hendricks," continued Caine, his back still to her, his shoulders tense, "I began divorce proceedings. Gwen was beside herself. She begged me to change my mind. Swore she loved me. Swore she'd end it. But I didn't want her to do that. I wanted out myself."

"That's understandable. Things end."

"But Gwen was no good at being on her own. I knew it, but I...I dismissed it—dismissed her—as not my problem anymore."

The tightness in Bella's chest increased. Was it any wonder he'd been so conflicted about being responsible for her these past days?

"She was a grown woman, Caine. She was responsible for her own choices."

He offered no reaction. "When Gwen realized I was serious, she ran straight to her Councilman." Caine's hands fisted by his side. "I warned her the bastard was no good. But she didn't listen. She insisted he would leave his wife for her. I don't doubt the guy made that promise. He was a lying snake who preyed on lonely soldiers' wives. But I couldn't get her to believe it."

"Stubborn, eh?" Bella cupped his shoulder, needing to touch him.

"Yeah. Like someone else I know." He turned his head, nuzzling her fingers with his jaw. "She went to him. Made a scene in front of the councilman's wife and a slew of other important dignitaries. Of course, Hendricks denied he even knew her. She must have been pretty pissed because she spewed personal details to prove him a liar. She also revealed he'd used Council funds for rendezvous for the two of them. He had her kicked out—and roughed up. She came to me, scared and crying. I told her to stay out of sight until I could get things figured out, but..." Caine shook his head, "she must have gone to see him. Two days later, she was found strangled to death in a trash dumpster close to my house. Word on the street was that Hendricks had his younger brother take her out. But no one was investigating the brother, much less the Councilman. There was another blight outbreak at the same time. People were focused on trying to survive."

"So you went after her killer?"

"I'd...I'd failed Gwen once. I couldn't do it again." He sucked in a deep breath. "But I wasn't planning on murder. I wanted Hendricks' brother to confess and go to prison. He was the one that came after me with a knife. Still, a part of me was glad. He'd murdered Gwen. I wanted him dead."

She pressed a kiss beneath his shoulder blade, gratified to feel a small tremble run through him. "You think that makes you a killer? I think it makes you a hero."

"What I did wasn't heroic, but I would have willingly paid the price for taking another killer's life. Only Gwen's councilman set me up, fingering me for crimes I never committed. Before long, I was branded a psychotic serial killer and sentenced to marooning on Dragath25."

"That's not going to happen again. You have allies now."

Caine swiveled around, his expression grim. "I had allies then, fighter girl. I was a decorated military hero with a lot of support from friends and family. I didn't matter. Hendricks paid off or ruined anyone who tried to defend me. He manufactured evidence so that it looked like I not only killed his brother, but Gwen and several other people who turned out to be enemies of the Councilman. He made me into the boogeyman and grew even more powerful. He's not going to let me back on Earth to tell his secret. I appreciate your optimism, fighter girl, but the only way I'm leaving Dragath25 is in a box."

"Don't say that." She grabbed his hand. "You might have had allies before, but you didn't have me. We didn't have the Oasis. Trust me, Caine. Please. Between the two of us, we're going to bring that corrupt bastard down. I swear it." She squeezed his palm. She had bigger plans as well, but she'd keep them to herself. "For you. For Gwen."

His expression remained bleak. "But if we can't, you're going. No argument."

She hid her hurt behind a joke. "Don't you know me well enough by now to know that will never happen?"

As hoped, his eyes crinkled in a half-smile, but his tone was serious. "That's why I like to call you fighter girl. Not because I don't see who you are, but because I do, Bella. I see exactly who you are. Someone extraordinary. Someone strong and kind. A true hero." His hands skimmed up her neck to cup her face. "Someone worth living for. Someone worth dying for."

His lips brushed hers. Reverent. Slow.

Her heart stuttered. He was kissing her. For the first time. Not for any deal. Or because he could. But because he wanted to. Because he was ready to let her in.

A low moan of need slipped from her. His words, his kiss, all she'd ever wanted.

As if the signal he'd been waiting for, the tenor of the kiss changed, his mouth claiming hers as his fingers wove through her hair and angled her closer. Her tongue tangled with his. His taste—of strength, ferocity, courage, hope—even better than she'd imagined.

When he finally drew back, his eyes still shut, their mouths only inches apart, their arms still latched around each other, they were both breathing hard.

Her heart fluttered. There it was again. That look of wonder on his face. As if she was something special. As if she was life itself.

Then his eyes sprang open. She stiffened, bracing for the change. For the return of the guarded look that had always entered his gaze before. But the tenderness remained.

"I didn't want to need you, Bella." His voice was a low rasp, his hands contracting against her skin. "I was terrified to need you. But somehow, somewhere, you've become a necessity. You've become everything. I might not trust anyone else, but I do trust you."

Her arms, locked around his neck, vibrated. It took her a moment to understand why. Caine was shaking. Like the first time they'd touched.

Awe whispered through her. This fierce warrior who'd fought off vicious beasts and killed for her was afraid. Because of his feelings for her.

"It's okay." She slid her hands to rest against his pounding chest. "I'll hold you together, just like you hold me. I swear." She pressed butterfly kisses to his chin, along his jaw. "I won't disappoint you, I promise. Because I need you, too." She swallowed hard. "Not for survival. Not for protection, but because of who are you. How you make me feel. As if I matter. As if I can do anything. As if I'm truly alive. And I love you for that, Caine. I do...."

Before she could even finish, his mouth was on hers again. Fierce. Wild. Desperate. His big hands glided over every inch of her. Touching her exactly as she loved to be touched. Until she was writhing against him. Until they were both naked and slick and ready. Until her legs were wrapped around his hips and she was whispering in his ear for him to take her. Her nipples tight. Her pussy wet and aching.

"We need a bed," he grouched. "I want this to be perfect."

She nipped at his jaw in warning. "I don't care where we are as long you're inside me in the next ten seconds."

His eyes crinkled as his lips turned upward. "So demanding." He laid her down on top of their clothing. The feel of him, hard and thick and ready at her entrance, made her moan. "We'll do perfect next time."

She lifted her hips to give him better access. "Don't you know by now? It's always perfect when I'm with you."

His smile dropped away, his expression turning so solemn she worried something might be wrong.

"You okay?"

He nodded. "Better than okay." Bracing his hands by her head, he came inside, slowly, worshipfully, inch by careful inch, until she was filled with him. "I love you so much, Bella."

Her pulse went crazy, her whole body flushing with white-hot pleasure. "You do?" Her question was whisper soft.

"I do." He flattened his palms against hers, interlacing their fingers as they had for their first touch. "I don't know what the future holds, but I do know nothing has ever felt as right as your hand in mine."

She was lost. Lost to the beauty of his words. Lost to the wonder of their connection. Lost to the exquisite, erotic bliss of him sliding in and out while their palms stayed sealed tight and every one of his fears and his shadows, his hopes and his needs, played across his face for her to see.

"Caine." She whispered his name, her legs wrapping around his waist, bringing them even closer.

"Bella." His mouth found hers, his gaze and hands her only anchor as a maelstrom of pleasure, fiercer than any dust storm, swirled through her, tightening her muscles and bowing her back as he drove deep, raw pleasure lashing at her.

Until his hips were moving at a fierce rate and she was moaning in his ear and their slick bodies writhed in tandem and they soared together over the edge, giving each other everything and anything—just as she'd promised so long ago.

Minutes later, her legs still wrapped around him, exquisite aftershocks coursed through her. They stared at one another, silly half smiles on their faces, wonder and awe floating around them like fairy dust.

When she finally got her breath back, she cradled his face in her palms. "We're getting out of here together."

His smile dissolved. "I'd like that," he said at last, "but shit happens. It's not going to be easy to get you, much less the two of us, off this planet. Even if my jammer does what I hope."

"You're not sacrificing yourself for me."

"Quality versus quantity, baby." He nuzzled her palm. "You gave me back myself. I'll be forever grateful to you for that."

She blinked hard and fast, that stupid stinging back in her eyes. "For a guy who rarely talks, sometimes you say the sweetest things....But I don't want your gratitude. I want you."

He smoothed his thumbs over the salty tracks rolling down her cheeks. She hadn't even realized she'd begun to cry.

He pressed his lips to hers. Slowly. Softly. "I never thought being sent to Dragath25 would be the best thing that ever happened to me, but there it is. You changed everything. If there's a way for me to come with you, I will."

Finally. "You promise?"

"I promise."

"Well, isn't this sweet." A grey barrel jammed against Caine's temple. Pogue loomed right behind. "But I'm afraid things might not work out for you lovebirds as planned."

CHAPTER TWENTY-ONE

"Put your hands up, Dragath25 scumbag, or you won't like the consequences." Pogue dug the gun muzzle deeper into Caine's skin. A ring of six soldiers stood behind him, their guns drawn, the glow from the lights strapped to their weapons giving their faces a menacing green tinge.

Bella's heart slammed against her ribs. "Put the gun down, Pogue." She injected as much command as possible into her voice. It wasn't easy with her breasts squashed against Caine's chest and her clothes strewn in a pile by the soldiers' boots. "He's on our side."

"I don't think so, Cadet West." There was no missing the sneer when Pogue referenced her title. Or the way his pupils were dilated, his gaze locked on her exposed skin. "What's going to happen is your boyfriend is going to move away from you nice and slow, or you're both going to end up feeling like you got socked by the sun up close and personal."

"Are you threatening to stun us?" Maybe she shouldn't have been shocked, but she was. "That's outrageous. We've done nothing wrong."

"Pogue," Caine's voice was a dangerous rasp, "give Cadet West her clothes. Then we'll move."

"You'll move now." Pogue's tone was smug. "It's not as if the rest of us haven't seen a pair of tits before—though those look to be mighty fine ones from up here." A low murmur of ugly laughter sounded from the ring of soldiers.

Her gaze locked with Caine's. "It's okay. Let me up." She swallowed hard. "It's only skin."

He stayed where he was, every muscle in his big body taut.

"Don't make him mad," she pleaded. "I don't want you hurt."

"Here." Her shirt fluttered into her line of vision, held out by a frowning Ransom.

She snaked her hand out fast. Her fingers trembling as she struggled into the shirt, her gaze locked with Caine's while Pogue yelled at Ransom for acting without an order.

She let out her first real breath when the long hem of Caine's shirt brushed against her lower thighs, infinitely grateful for its length.

"No more stalling," snapped Pogue.

"Relax," Caine told Pogue, "I'm not planning on giving you any trouble—as long as you don't bother Bella." Expression solemn, he kissed the tip of her nose. "It will be okay." He levered himself up, push-up style, pulling her to stand behind him before Pogue and his soldiers had time to react.

There were seven guns trained on Caine in the next instant.

"You cooperate and there'll be no problems." Pogue shifted his gun to lock on her forehead. "You give us trouble and she'll suffer the consequences."

Caine gave a low growl.

"Officer Pogue, this is absolutely unnecessary." Winthrop, who she hadn't even realized was there, stepped from behind one of the soldiers, his face pale, his gaze not quite meeting hers. "Cadet West is our colleague."

"*Was* our colleague," challenged Pogue, his tone absent of any deference as he contradicted Winthrop. "She's with the enemy now."

Clearly, the disappearance of the two crew members had flipped a switch inside Pogue, emboldening him even further in his break from protocol and his claim of leadership. It couldn't have happened at a worse time.

"We're no one's enemies," she said. "We're on your side."

"Then why'd you pick off Davies and Pratt?" barked Pogue.

"We didn't do anything to them."

"Remove the gun aimed at Bella." As always, Caine sounded in complete control. "We can answer your questions and resolve this without anyone getting hurt."

She knew he was holding back from fighting in an effort to protect her.

"Put your hands behind your back." Pogue's voice was brusque.

"I will, as a gesture of good faith." Caine's muscles bunched as he did as requested. "I expect you to behave accordingly with Bella."

Pogue said nothing. Uncertainty skittered through her. Were they doing the right thing by trying to talk some sense into Winthrop, Pogue, and the others? It hadn't worked so far. But finding Ava was more likely with their help and, equally significant, there was no getting Caine off this hellhole if they didn't have the support of at least Winthrop.

"You see, Dr. Winthrop?" She purposely directed her attention to him. "Caine is cooperating. He's on our side."

Winthrop nodded, but he didn't speak. One of the soldiers stepped forward and snapped a pair of Council restraints on Caine's wrists. As usual, the restraints expanded, encasing Caine's arms from wrist to forearm.

"Feel familiar, convict?" mocked Pogue.

"Don't talk to him like that." Bella could barely breathe over the dread coursing through her. Appeasement wasn't calming Pogue. In fact, it seemed to be having the opposite effect. "He'd done what you wanted. Now back off and let us explain."

"You're right, Bella," mocked Pogue. "I apologize for talking to your precious convict like that." Without warning, he slammed the barrel of his gun between Caine's shoulder blades. "He understands violence better."

"No!" She leapt forward, only to be snapped back as Mitchell, Pogue's second-in-command, wrapped his arm around her waist and lifted her off the ground.

But if they thought that was all it would take, they were mistaken. Using Caine's training, she curled into a squat, dragging the bastard off balance, and smashed her boot down on his foot. His arms fell away on a howl.

"I said get away from him." She ran at Pogue. The time for appeasement had come to an end. But, just as she reached him, she was knocked off-course, lifted sideways by an enraged Mitchell and another soldier.

She heard Caine's roar. Heard the shout of other soldiers and the crunch of bone as Caine fought to get to her, but it was no use. They had guns. His arms were restrained behind his back. And her training wasn't enough against a greater number of skilled soldiers. Even fighting like a madwoman, channeling Caine's techniques, lips pulled back in a sneer, she was soon contained.

Her breath came in furious pants as Mitchell wrapped her in a bear hug and the other soldier grasped her legs, holding her off the ground, restrained between them. She could do little more than wriggle. And blink as the slow drip of blood from a new cut seeped into her eye. Or maybe the blood was from Mitchell? She'd definitely gotten in a few good strikes.

But it hadn't been enough.

Her heart shriveled as she took in Caine. Unlike her, he'd been winning. There were a few new bruises on his face and chest, but he stood tall and free around a ring of writhing, fallen soldiers. Pogue, unfortunately, wasn't one of them.

"Don't hurt her." Caine had stopped fighting.

"Go, Caine. Run," she screamed.

But the stubborn man remained where he was. "I won't fight back. Just don't hurt her."

"Worry for yourself." Eyes glittering with fury, Pogue drove his gun barrel into Caine, driving him to his knees.

"Stop it!" She bucked against Mitchell's hold, wanting to tear apart every soldier there with her bare hands.

"Maybe you should have thought of that before you fought back?" Pogue drew his boot back and kicked Caine in the stomach, the kick so hard it sent Caine sliding back several lengths.

The other soldiers stumbled to their feet, uncertain, their expressions ranging from discomfort to glee.

"Winthrop, order him to stop." She searched for the Councilman she'd once admired in the light of the glow sticks and found him standing frozen, a look of horror on his face. "Caine was helping me look for Ava. He's only ever tried to help." This was her fault. She'd brought Caine into contact with these monsters. "You're beating an innocent man."

Winthrop shifted his weight from one boot to the next, his expression uncertain. Afraid. As if without protocol, without the trappings of Command Council, he was lost. "Pogue, perhaps you should—"

"He's a dangerous criminal," snarled Pogue, cutting off Winthrop and kicking Caine again, his beautiful body jerking forward with the force of the hit. "He's brainwashed Cadet West." Another kick. "He's a danger to us and the Council." Pogue bent over, sweat from his temple splashing onto Caine's still body. "Tell us what you did with Pratt and Davies, Dragath25 scum, or you won't like what happens next."

She couldn't see Caine's face. Didn't know if he was even still conscious. He hadn't made a sound from the start of the beating. He wasn't talking now, either.

"He didn't do anything," she yelled. "He's trying to find them. Plus, he's found a way to save the rescue crew. He's a hero, and you bastards are going to be tried for attacking him."

Pogue just laughed. "Wow. He fucked the smarts right out of you. You think it's any coincidence he shows up right around the time Pratt and Davies disappeared? Check around and we'll probably find he's made their skin into some nice new Dragath25 accessory."

"That's sickening. Caine would never do that."

"Oh yeah? We found evidence of his base camp near ours. Fucker's been stalking us for a while."

"He wasn't stalking anyone. He was watching out for me. Protecting me."

"Riiight." Pogue's voice was heavy with sarcasm. "Because you actually matter to him beyond a nice tight hole he can stick into when he has the urge." His fellow soldiers laughed again.

She slammed her head back against the chuckling bastard holding her arms behind her back. Stopped his laughter quite nicely. On the negative side, though, it sent a vicious pain winding down her skull and neck. She had to blink slowly to stop the ringing.

"The bitch broke my nose," her captor howled.

"Don't like it? Let me go." She thrashed in earnest, her ribs close to snapping under the punishing grip of her captor's hold. The soldier grasping her legs had gone pale.

"Bella, calm down." Caine's low command sent relief spiraling through her. He was alive. And conscious.

He pushed to his knees, turning to face her. "I've taken a lot worse, believe me. Don't give them a reason to hurt you."

She let out a sob. Blood ran down the side of his face. His beautiful, strong jaw was already beginning to swell.

So far she was doing a crappy job of protecting him.

"I'm sorry," she told him. "I should never have asked for your help. I should never have offered you that deal. You were doing just fine on your own. I…I've made everything so much worse."

His expression grew hard. "Finding you was the best thing that happened to me. Don't forget it." His gaze shifted to Pogue. "Anyone who harms a hair on her head will be dead by tomorrow."

Even on his knees, he was so sure and proud. So full of command and dignity. Her chest grew tight. He truly was an amazing man.

"You really think you're some kind of hero, don't you?" Pogue's laugh chilled Bella's blood. "You're nothing but a scumbag convict. No one cares if one more Dragath25 prisoner dies." He shoved the gun against Caine's back and pressed the lever.

Hundreds of volts of vicious electricity poured through Caine's body, all the more visible against the backdrop of the dark night. He dropped to the ground, his eyes sinking shut, his body shuddering under the assault.

"No!" She fought with everything she had.

Pogue lifted the stun gun off Caine and pointed it in her direction. "You need to calm down or you'll be deemed as a threat to our survival and treated just like your enemy lover."

"Fuck you!" She kept fighting.

"That's enough." Winthrop had made his way to the front now.

"Stay out of this, Winthrop," growled Pogue "We may need to keep you alive, but you're not in charge any more. This situation now falls under the realm of a threat to our survival. My territory."

Winthrop's hand flew to his neck as if to check that the Command Council brand was still there. His mouth opened, but no words came out.

"The bitch deserves what she gets." Mitchell filled the silence, aping his leader's example while still holding her in a painful grip. "If you lay with animals, you get treated like one."

Only Ransom and Winthrop didn't nod in agreement.

"Always said I wanted to see this particular one tied up and restrained." Pogue's smile was terrifying.

She forced herself not to rise to their bait. "This is still a Council mission." Her gaze locked on Caine, taking heart from the steady rise and fall of his chest. "Winthrop, you are the highest ranking officer here. You can decide what happens next." Reaching him was her only hope. "Not because you're Council, but because you're a good man who knows what's right. Just because we're on Dragath25 doesn't mean we do away with order and justice."

"I'm in charge now," roared Pogue. "Not him. Not the Council. Me!"

"Winthrop," she pleaded, "don't let this happen. It's not right. You came here to save humanity. You risked your life for what you thought was right. Don't tarnish that now. Don't let us become nothing more than beasts."

Winthrop took a defiant step toward Pogue. Then Winthrop's gaze landed on the hard stares of the other soldiers, and he took an instinctual shuffle step back, curling into himself, adrift without the mantle of Council entitlement. He held out his hands, palms up in a placating gesture that had bile rising in the back of Bella's throat. "I don't...this—this is silly." His gaze met neither hers nor Pogue's. "We all need to just take a deep breath and think things through. Bella can come with me while you question the prisoner. We're all just trying to do the right thing here."

Disappointment slammed through her. Winthrop was burying his head in the sand again. "I'm not leaving Caine."

"For once, she's right." Pogue stalked toward Caine's pack "You're not leaving here with her," he told Winthrop, "and I don't need more time." He ripped open the pack and rummaged around inside.

Dread twisted Bella's stomach.

"Surprise, surprise." Pogue pulled out a heap of twisted wires and wreckage. "A weapon." He held it toward

Winthrop, shaking it in his grasp, sending wires flailing. "He wants to kill us all, and she's trying to protect him."

"No," she protested. "He built that to help us. I told you before our shuttle was brought down by a prison gang. They intend to do the same thing to the rescue shuttle. Caine built that to jam their weapon and save those people. Save us."

"Bullshit," snarled Pogue, but the rest of his words died as a roar sounded overheard. Way up high and off to the left, a tiny metallic disc flashed in the otherwise black sky.

"Holy shit. It's the rescue shuttle." Pogue dropped Caine's jammer into the dirt. "We're saved."

Bella's heart leapt—and then took a shuddering dive. Her gaze shot to the jumble of wires by Pogue's boots. "We need to use Caine's machine. Otherwise, those people are going to die."

Unfortunately, no one was listening. Everyone was too busy shouting and pointing toward the growing flickering lights overhead.

Seizing her chance, she kicked out, sending the distracted soldier holding her legs stumbling back. Knocked off kilter, Mitchell released her with a curse.

She landed hard on her ass. Scrambling forward, she dodged her captor's grasp and crawled to Caine, rolling him over. Her chest loosened as she took in the rise and fall of his chest.

"Caine?" She fumbled frantically for the catch that would release his restraints, "Can you hear me, baby? We need to—"

A rough arm lifted her up and away before she could complete her task.

"I don't think so." Pogue's hot breath rasped against her ear. "Time to say goodbye to your boyfriend, Cadet West. You want a good fucking once we're back in space, I'll be glad to show you what a real man can do."

Before she could take a swing, he hitched her higher in his arms, squeezing so hard black dots danced in front of her eyes. She dug her nails into his skin, but it had little impact. Without breath, she couldn't even scream, much less fight.

He pitched his voice to be heard by his men over the growing roar. "We need to get back to the clearing so the shuttle can land. Let's get the fuck off this hellhole."

"No, we...need that...machine. We need...Caine." Wheezing, flailing, she thrashed in Pogue's hold while her gaze locked with Winthrop's. "Otherwise, those people...are going to die...and...it will be...our fault."

Winthrop paled. Pogue ignored her.

She sucked down a desperate breath. "You can't...just leave him here."

As if she weighed no more than a child, Pogue threw her over his shoulder. "He's a fucking scumbag criminal. You'll be thanking us soon enough for saving you. He was never going to do anything but die here on this planet anyway."

Kicking, clawing, she fought for release, but it was no good. Against some of the other men, she might have had a chance. But not Pogue.

"Caine!" She was still fighting. She was still screaming his name as Pogue sprinted down the hill, the other soldiers following close behind, Caine's unmoving body all too soon disappearing from sight.

CHAPTER TWENTY-TWO

The low rumble of the shuttle's motors shifted to a frantic whir.

"Shit! They're falling." Pogue jerked to a stop in the clearing, his voice tight with disbelief. All around her, the other soldiers had stumbled to a halt, too.

"Because their equipment is being jammed. Just like ours." She was too horrified to feel righteous rage. Good people, who'd come to save them, were about to die. "Let me go." She pushed against Pogue's back. Almost in a daze, he set her on her feet, his gaze locked on the dropping ship.

She shifted in place, torn between trying to make it back to Caine and doing what she could to help those who'd come to save her.

A series of shrill shrieks echoed across the cliffs raising goose bumps.

Of course. 225 and his pack were coming for their prize. Just as they'd done last time.

"We've got to hide." Pogue's face had lost all color, his gaze scanning left and right as he gripped his gun tight.

"And leave any crash survivors to those monsters?" She had to scream now to be heard over the roar of the plummeting shuttle. "The people on that shuttle were coming to save you. You can't just desert them."

He shook her off, turning toward his men. "Let's go."

To their credit, the other six soldiers stayed put. Their gazes flickering to the listing, spinning shuttle, its Council Search and Rescue stamp easy to see in the shuttle flood lights as it roared closer and closer to the ground.

"Sir?" Ransom questioned Pogue, "maybe she's right."

"Do you know what those animals will do to us if they find us?" snarled Pogue. "I'm not going out like that."

Her potential ally folded in on himself, Ransom's pupils widening as fear won.

The pounding of footsteps from the way they'd come sent the soldiers whipping around, their guns clenched tight.

Winthrop appeared from behind a rocky ledge, his pace slow, his face flushed. "Shit. Bella was right. The shuttle's going to crash." He bent over as if the run had given him a stitch in his side. "I'm sorry," he wheezed. "We should have believed you."

She wasn't in a forgiving mood. She swiped at the blood dripping into her eye. "You should have believed Caine."

Guilt flared in Winthrop's gaze. "You're right."

Pogue grabbed Winthrop's arm. "Save the sucking up for later. We're out of here."

Another set of shrieks sounded, closer than before.

"No." Winthrop shook Pogue off. "Listening to you was wrong. You're not in charge. I am."

Somehow, faced with the consequences of his cowardice, Winthrop had found his backbone. Only it was too late.

The shuttle was coming in fast now, only a few hundred yards up and off to the left, its nose pointed downward, close enough to the ground to see the underside of the shuttle even as it spun, its engines sputtering and sparking as whatever was jamming it kept everything from working properly. So close, the roar of its descent was as loud as a scream of agony in her ear.

It was horrific to realize she knew exactly what those poor people inside the shuttle were feeling. How terror was gripping their chests as all the regrets, all the people they loved, all the things they'd never get to do played through their minds. She swayed on her feet, memories of her own crash blurring with her guilt and pain over what she was seeing now.

Then, suddenly, she blinked, her eyes disbelieving.

It...it almost seemed as if the engines were streaming to life. As if the sparking embers had become one long continual flame.

"He did it." Winthrop's voice was heavy with awe. Beside him, Pogue had gone still.

In shock, her stare returned to the shuttle. It was still coming in far too fast, but it had stabilized somewhat, its nose no longer pointed downward.

Caine had done it.

"How?" she whispered.

"I heard what you had to say." Winthrop grabbed her hand. "I doubled back to release him. Not because I'm Council and my order should be followed, but because it was the right thing to do. I wanted him to come with me, but he insisted on trying to get the equipment to work."

"Is he okay?" Her throat was so tight it was hard to get the words out.

"He's fine. A real hero."

"Tell that to the Council," she said. "Please."

"I will."

They instinctively ducked as the shuttle, struggling for control, thundered overhead. Close enough that the heat of the engines singed their skin and its roar deafened their ears. It bowled into the hard rocky ground, debris spewing everywhere as it tore forward several metrals into the planet's surface, its wheels digging for traction. Then it spun to the side, smacked into the cliff, and shuddered to a halt.

Alarms whirred. Sparks flew from one engine. But the shuttle was intact. Hope poured through Bella. Caine had really and truly done it. Against all odds, he'd saved the people on that shuttle.

Floodlights flashed on, lighting up the valley.

In the next heartbeat, the shuttle door lowered. Grey gun barrels poked through the entrance, followed by big men in familiar Council soldier uniforms. They fanned out and started marching in their direction.

Help had arrived.

"Thank God," whispered Winthrop. "And thank Caine."

Bella had to agree. He'd done it. He'd saved them all.

She turned back the way they'd come. Pogue and the other soldiers were already sprinting toward the rescuers, calling out the identification codes that would prove them survivors of the crash.

A hand clasped her arm. "Where are you going?" Winthrop's troubled gaze met hers.

"I'm going to find Caine. I can't leave him here." The screeches were so loud and frequent now, they were a constant feral hum. "We'll hide in the caves until the prisoners leave."

"You'll never make it back up the hill before those prisoners arrive."

"I have to try."

Winthrop's eyes sunk shut. When they opened, they were filled with determination—and sorrow. "I'm sorry, Bella."

"What's wrong?" She didn't like the look on Winthrop's face.

"He made me promise." Before she could make sense of Winthrop's words, her already sore stomach took a hit as his shoulder plowed into her and her world turned upside down.

"No!" She struggled to right herself.

Not as strong as Caine or Pogue, Winthrop staggered under her assault, but he managed to stay upright. "He made me swear I'd get you to safety." His voice was laced with strain. "Said I could make things right if I get you on that shuttle, no matter what."

Didn't Caine understand that there would be no making it right for her if he wasn't there?

"No. He has to come, too." Slamming her palms into the vulnerable area just over Winthrop's kidney, she dropped back to her feet as he doubled-over with a howl. "Sorry, Winthrop." She scrambled backwards. "You left me no choice." Pivoting, she screamed toward the hills. "Caine, I'm not leaving here without you." She had no idea if he could hear her over 225's pack. Still, she had to try. "You promised!"

"He's a survivor, Bella." Winthrop called out to her as she moved farther away. "He'll be okay. We can send someone back for him later."

"It will be too late," she shouted back. "The pack will know he's the one who helped us. They'll destroy him. Stall as best you can." He'd saved her. She would save him, too. "I'll be back with him as soon as possible."

"Freeze," barked an unfamiliar voice. "Identify yourself."

A lean guy in a Council uniform stood behind Winthrop, the latest in Council weaponry, something that looked like a cross between a gun and a computer in his hand. He looked decidedly uneasy.

She froze. "I need to go."

The soldier in Council uniform hitched his gun higher.

"You're not going anywhere." Pogue and the other soldiers closed in around her.

"Thank you for coming." Ignoring her, Winthrop approached the soldier from the rescue shuttle. He was talking fast as he held out his wrist for the scan. "All accounted for. Let's move out."

The lean guy's scanner beeped, but he didn't relax. "Her, too?"

"Her, too."

Fury whipped through her. She wanted to run, but she was afraid the soldier would shoot her. The instant he was distracted, however,....

"We were told there were thirty-seven crewmembers on board the last shuttle." Disbelief laced the soldier's voice. "Are you saying you're all that's left?"

"No," she protested, "there are critical personnel missing."

"Don't listen to her," snapped Pogue. "Dragath25 prisoners are closing in fast. We need to get out of here."

"What the hell is that?" Eyes wide, the rescue soldier pointed behind her.

She swiveled back around, horror rising in the back of her throat. She'd missed her chance.

Like locusts, hundreds of shrieking prisoners swarmed over the cliff, pouring into the clearing as if unleashed from the bowels of the planet. Dirty, wild, most in little more than rags. Some carried spears, some twisted wreckage. In the flickering light of the shuttle flood lamps, all had the wild, deadly look of rabid animals crazed by blood lust.

Nausea spread through her. *Please, please*, she prayed, *please let Caine be safe and beyond their reach.*

"Holy shit," whispered Winthrop. "They're going to tear us apart."

There was no more time to look for Caine. No time even to hide in the caves.

"Run," shouted one of the rescue team. "Get to the shuttle."

But before anyone could move, a stream of red light cut through the air, followed by a scream, the stench of burned flesh. The officer to her left fell to the ground. Mitchell crumpled next.

"They have guns," shouted another rescue team soldier, firing back. "Protect the survivors. Defensive positions." Unlike Pogue and his team, this team of soldiers was well-trained and courageous. They instantly circled around her and the rest of her colleagues.

225's pack had guns. Where had they gotten guns?

Winthrop must have been wondering the same thing because he whirled to face Pogue. "You said the lost soldiers' guns were destroyed."

Pogue's silence spoke for itself.

Another beam of light flashed. Another rescue soldier went down.

Chaos ensued. Another team member fell. One of Pogue's men dropped, too. She tripped over his leg, but managed to right herself.

"We'll never make it," shouted one of the remaining rescuers, his expression resigned. She knew that look. She'd seen the same one on Caine.

"Shoot," the man ordered into his wrist transmission, communicating with the crew still on board the shuttle. "It's the only chance we've got. They'll overrun us and the shuttle otherwise."

In the next instance, flashes of light streamed from the shuttle, trapping her and her colleagues between two dangers. Most of the shuttle beams went over their head and into the crazed crowd beyond, felling many of the frontline, but one shot went astray, slamming into the very rescue soldier who'd just given the order. He went down hard, victim to friendly fire.

There was no time to even mourn.

"Stay low," she shouted to Winthrop. "If we can make it a few more paces, we'll be below the arc line." She cast a quick glance in his direction. As expected, his face was drenched in sweat, his face twisted in pain. That he'd been able to make it this far was a miracle given his injuries.

She risked another quick glance over her shoulder. She shouldn't have looked.

The shuttle lasers had taken out a huge chunk of the frontline, but too many prisoners had managed to avoid being hit. They surged forward as the lasers recharged. Another rescue soldier went down, not by lasers this time, but by hands.

Her mind could barely process the terrified scream of the soldier as the pack closed in, ripping at his skin, his limbs, his eyes.

Bile rose in her throat. She could only pray the poor man was already dead.

"Keep running!" Her command snapped Winthrop back into action.

"Help," Ransom screamed as he was dragged down by two prisoners. Pogue didn't even look back.

She was turning to help when a vicious force slammed into her.

CHAPTER TWENTY-THREE

Bella hit the ground hard, her chin slamming into the dirt. She blinked back the fog as hands clawed at her, flipping her over. A dark-haired man with one grey eye and a puckered scar loomed overhead.

"Gotcha," he leered.

She swung, but he was faster. Her head twisted sideways as his brutal punch rocked her cheek. His hands tore at her thighs. She raised her fists to fight back when her attacker toppled. Winthrop stood above.

He stuck out his hand. "Come on."

Dizzy, grateful, she reached for his hand. Only to have it wrenched away as another prisoner plowed into Winthrop, slamming him to the ground. Another hard weight crashed into her, stealing the breath from her lungs.

Rough hands raked at her flesh, pinching, slashing. Too many for her to fight at once. She tried to curl up in a ball, but they were pulling at her limbs, grasping at her skin. Her ankle snapped. She screamed in agony. Tried to picture Caine's face. Tried to remember better times. Joy. Pleasure. All that she'd had.

Her legs were wrenched apart. Fabric ripped.

Then a roar sounded, louder even than the prisoners' shrieks.

The press of bodies disappeared.

She blinked. Certain she was dreaming.

Caine, blood running down his face, his chest lashed with cuts, loomed above. A pile of bodies surrounded him.

He'd come for her.

He drove his spear into the nearest body. Then another. Until no one around her or Winthrop moved.

"Hold on." Caine reached down and scooped her up, cradling her against his chest as he ran. Winthrop limped right behind.

She didn't ask how Caine had found her or bother protesting that he put her down. She couldn't run, and she knew he wouldn't leave her. They'd only lose precious time arguing. Instead, she surveyed the path to the shuttle and shouted out a warning whenever a prisoner approached. Holding her breath as Caine's spear whizzed through the air, cutting down anyone who tried to stop them. Whatever happened next, she was just glad to have Caine close, his warm skin pressed against hers, his steady heartbeat thumping in time with hers.

Still, the pounding of his boots on the gangplank was the sweetest sound she'd ever heard.

"Don't shoot. We're the good guys." Winthrop waved his arms over his head, seeking to calm the guards manning the gangplank. They'd been mowing down any prisoners who got too close. "Council mission D25642."

Hope washed over her. They were going to make it.

Then a flash of light, a grunt from Caine, and his hold loosened. She gasped, clutching at his shoulder as she started to fall, but he managed to regain his grip, hoisting her higher. "Don't worry." His steady voice was a whisper in her ear. "I got you, fighter girl."

She was about to smile when Winthrop's words made her blood run cold. "You're hit."

"Where?" Panicking, she ran her palms over Caine's chest, searching for a wound. "Put me down. You shouldn't be carrying me. I can make it. We can make it together."

"It's a scratch. Nothing to worry about." But he let her slide down his body.

Blood dripped from his thigh. There wasn't time to attend to it. Not with the shrieks of the attacking prisoners growing ever closer.

Slipping under his shoulder to offer support, she and Caine limped the last few steps up the gangplank toward the shuttle door. Winthrop right behind. The two guards covering their backs.

Suddenly, Pogue appeared in the doorway. "Not him." He pointed his gun at Caine. "He's one of them. A filthy Dragath25 prisoner. Throw him back."

"No," she protested, stepping in front of Caine. "You can't." She was pulled behind him in the next second.

Winthrop was yelling at the same time. "This man's a hero. He's with us."

Uncertain, the guards' weapons swung back and forth between Caine and Pogue. They had seconds to make a decision before the next wave of prisoners stormed the gangplank.

"He saved me from being torn apart," she insisted. "He saved you, too."

Thankfully, the rescue soldier's weapon landed back on Pogue.

"Put down your gun," the soldier told Pogue. "We're all coming aboard."

"You're taking a criminal's word over mine?" Enraged, Pogue pressed the trigger. "I'm the hero, not him."

"No!" Bella screamed.

But it was too late.

Even as the soldier's weapon fire slammed into Pogue and he toppled from the gangplank, his gun discharged, slicing through skin and muscle. The acrid scent of burnt flesh tinged the air.

Winthrop crumpled to the ground.

He'd leapt in front of Caine.

"No." Bella dropped to her knees, her hand hovering over the gaping wound that had once been her superior's chest, afraid her touch would only hurt him more. "Don't—

don't move. It's going to be alright." She'd wanted him to get all he wanted. She'd wanted to see him save Earth and find the right girl like he'd always dreamed. She wanted him to be the leader he always could have been.

"Even...even you can't...save me this time." Winthrop's voice was a weak rasp, his smile sad and kind, just as when she'd sat beside him on that metal bench so long ago. "At least...I got to be a hero, after all." His words grew fainter as his eyes sunk shut. "Find Ava.....she deserves a hero, too."

Bella hadn't realized she was sobbing until she tried to speak. No words came out.

Then there was no more time as another prisoner leapt on the gangplank. Two more right behind.

"We have to go." As if choreographed, Caine scooped her up, handing her off to one of the other soldiers. He slung Winthrop over his shoulders. "We're not leaving him behind."

The other soldiers seemed to understand. Without another word, they shielded Caine's back, guarding Winthrop's body as they crossed the threshold into the shuttle.

"Survivors retrieved," hollered one of the rescue team as they stumbled inside. "Shut the doors. STAT."

Bella's boots vibrated at the shuttle rose, the doors still closing. The screaming below faded over the roar of the engines. The calm, methodical whir of the ship was disorienting after so much chaos. Dazed, she slumped against the metal shuttle wall, balancing gingerly on her one good ankle.

Out of thirty-five crew, only she had made it back alive. Winthrop was dead. Ava still missing. A sob ran through her. Then her gaze found Caine.

He was gently passing Winthrop off to two soldiers.

Her heart leapt. Yes, there'd been too much death, too much waste of good life, but something wonderful had happened, too. Caine had made it off Dragath25 alive.

At least for the moment.

It didn't escape her notice that two soldiers' guns remained trained on him, their gazes wary.

"Put your guns down," she insisted. "He's the one who saved your lives. Without him, your engines would have stayed jammed and you'd be down there defenseless against those monsters."

A stern-faced man with salt and pepper hair, a crisp Council uniform, and a Captain insignia stepped forward. "Is that true?" His question was for Caine.

"I was able to create a jammer from spare parts to counteract the machine that brought the other shuttle down, Sir." In his rapid, no-nonsense response, it was easy to hear the soldier Caine had always been.

"And who are you, ma'am?" The Captain asked her, his assessing gaze traveling the length of her.

She tugged at her hem, suddenly well aware that she was in nothing but Caine's big, old-fashioned shirt. No official Council uniform in sight.

Putting as much steel into her spine as she could muster, she offered an official Council salute. "I'm Cadet West. One of the junior scientists under Dr. Winthrop," she managed to say his name with only a tremble, "assigned to the previous research mission to Dragath25. When our shuttle crashed, Caine saved my life. He did the same for a number of other colleagues as well."

"So this man here is a prisoner and not mission personnel?"

She exchanged a quick glance with Caine. If he wanted her to handle this differently, he wasn't giving her any clue.

"That's right," she admitted. "But his initial sentence was a crime in itself and his efforts these past two weeks saved not only my life, but the life of your crew."

Painful seconds ticked by while the Captain considered her words. Finally, he nodded, his gaze locking with Caine's. "Seems we owe you our thanks."

She let out a deep breath. Especially when the guns trained on Caine dropped.

"I'd like Cadet West to be examined by a doctor," Caine said, "and then we can discuss what you want to do about me."

"Do about you?" she echoed. "There's no question. You need to be looked at, too, Caine. You've been shot. Then we're going back to the space station and then to Earth, and we'll make sure the world knows what you've done for us today."

"One thing at a time," said the Captain—his gaze flickering between them as if trying to ascertain the exact nature of their relationship. "You both look pretty banged up. Medics will see to both of you. Then they'll show you to some quarters where you can get cleaned up and rest. But tomorrow morning at eight hundred hours, I expect you in my quarters. I'll need a full report. A lot of people are going to be wondering just what the hell happened here. Especially why I'm bringing back a Dragath25 prisoner as one of my only survivors."

"We'll be there," answered Caine, his warning stare restraining her from saying anything more.

The Captain started to step aside so the medics could do their work. He stopped suddenly. "There was a lot of hope for Earth's future riding on your mission, Cadet West. Any chance you have good news?"

"Yes." It was a wonderful feeling to be able to give such an answer—and her chest squeezed again as she wished Winthrop and Ava were there to give it with her. "Our mission offered some real possibilities for making Earth habitable and healthy once again." She took a deep breath, "I intend to make sure every bit of that information is passed onto the Command Council—once I'm assured everything with Caine has been squared away."

The Captain's eyebrows rose. Off to the side, she heard Caine issue her name in a warning growl. She didn't care.

He'd protected her and her colleagues as best as he could. Now it was her turn to do the same for him.

CHAPTER TWENTY-FOUR

The rumble of voices in the hallway woke Bella. She sat up, her heart beating fast, her gaze taking in the gleaming metal walls of the sparse ship quarters, the empty bunk beds to her left and right, the half lit artificial lighting that never turned completely off, and her clean, new Council uniform.

She hadn't been dreaming. She and Caine had really made it off Dragath25 alive.

Careful not to knock her ankle cast, she rose awkwardly and limped toward the door. The medics had finished fixing her up far faster than Caine. After a shower and some food, she'd lain down on the bed to wait for him. Obviously, she'd fallen asleep.

That he hadn't come to wake her only made her more uneasy.

Her door slid open with the press of her palm. Caine stood across the hall, two Council guards flanking him. Obviously, the Captain still wasn't quite sure what to make of him. She'd been shadowed by guards as well, but they'd left her once they'd brought her to her quarters. Caine's appeared intent on sticking around.

"Hey," she said, leaning against the doorframe for support. Showered and dressed in someone's loaner Council uniform, his clothes emphasizing every inch of his broad shoulders and long legs, Caine looked unbelievably handsome—and more removed from her than ever.

"You're up," he turned toward her, leaving the guards in front of his door, his usual graceful gait marred by a slight limp. Still, the medics had done a good job. All his cuts and bruises had been treated and his laser wound dressed. His gaze traveled from her head to toe. "You okay? The medics refused to tell me about your condition."

That he'd asked went far toward soothing her worries.

"I'm fine. Just a bad ankle sprain." She reached up and rubbed away a water droplet that clung stubbornly to his spiky hair. He sucked in a harsh breath, his eyes hungry. The moment reminded her of the first time she'd really seen him. When he'd dunked himself in that first cave and revealed the man beneath. It was amazing to think how badly she'd come to want that man to be hers. Not just for short-term protection, but for a lifetime of whatever life chose to send their way. He'd become her world. "What about you? How's your leg?"

"Just a scratch."

She hadn't expected him to say anything else.

A heavy silence fell between them.

She could see the concern in his gaze. But there was something else, too. The same wariness he'd had when they first met.

She eyed the guards. They were kindly trying to appear as if they weren't listening.

"You want to come in?" she asked Caine. She didn't care where the Captain thought Caine should sleep. She wanted him with her.

He stilled, as if she'd surprised him. "Probably not the best idea. We, ah...we should probably give it some time."

Was there anything more painful than a guy who didn't want to hurt your feelings? Still, she wasn't about to run from the truth. After Dragath25, she knew she could handle anything.

"Give what some time?" she pushed. "If things have changed now that we're heading back to Earth and you don't want to be with me anymore, just say it."

She wasn't going to let him do that distance, all-business thing again. Last time, he'd said he'd done it because he was afraid of losing her, but that excuse wouldn't fly now. She was standing right here. Available for a lifetime. If only he'd reach out and touch her.

His big hands closed around her forearms. "Of course I want to be with you."

"Sir?" One of the guards spoke. The other was already reaching for his weapon. "Is there a problem here?"

Caine tensed, but he didn't drop his hands. "No problem at all." His voice was an angry rumble. "Can we get a minute?"

It had to be weird to have to answer to others after eight years of being entirely on your own.

"We're fine," she seconded, knowing the guards would need to hear it from her, too. "We'll talk inside my room. It will be less awkward for all."

The guards exchanged an uncertain look.

"Please. It won't matter if you stand outside my room or his," she coaxed, "as long as you're keeping watch." She'd been dealing with Council protocol her whole life. She knew how to work around it when necessary.

Neither guard looked particularly happy, but they didn't protest as Caine walked her backward through her doorway, the door sliding closed with a definite whoosh.

They stared at each other in silence.

"You say you want to be with me," she said at last, "so why are you pulling away?"

"I'm not pulling away." He looked frustrated. "I just...I want to give you some time to make sure I'm what you want. The way those guards reacted...the way people are going to see me...that's how it's always going to be if you stay with me." He shook his head. "We're not on Dragath25 now. You have choices."

She should have known. But that's what you got when you fell for a real hero.

She moved closer, pressing her body against his, her arms slipping around his waist. "It wouldn't matter where in the universe we were. You are exactly what I want, Caine. You. No one else."

He swallowed hard. His arms remained by his side. "If I'd been any kind of real man, there wouldn't have been a deal between us from the start."

His words hit like a punch. "I don't understand." She didn't want him to regret their deal. Being with him was the only good thing that had come out of crash landing on Dragath25.

"I saw you. I wanted you. So I took. I told myself it was the Dragath25 way. It wasn't right."

Now, she understood. Guilt was eating at him. Making him question whether he deserved a better ending than a lonely death on Dragath25.

"Should I feel guilty, too?" she asked, her palms curling against his chest, the steady pounding of his heart comforting beneath her hand. "I didn't know you, but I asked you to risk your life for me and my colleagues. I bartered on your good will and your loneliness. I took and took."

"No." His hands curled around her shoulders. "You gave me so much."

"Then we're even." She stared into his eyes, willing him to see things her way. "It was a fair deal. Don't make yourself out to be the bad guy when you weren't. It was something good. For both of us. Don't regret it." Her voice cracked. "Please."

A firm hand gripped her chin. "I could never regret being with you. Ever."

Relief whispered through her. "I love you, Caine." She couldn't keep it inside for another second. She needed to tell him again. Needed to hear him tell her, too. Now. When they were off Dragath25 and anything was possible.

She held her breath.

He pressed his forehead to hers, his eyes crinkling in that sweet, sexy way. "I never thought I'd say that ending up on Dragath25 was the best thing that happened to me, but every single one of those miserable eight years was worth it since I met you." He cradled her face in his hands. "You're everything to me, fighter girl. I'd die for you."

"But will you live for me, too? Will you fight whatever's coming to be with me?"

"I told you. I love you. Plain and simple. If you want to be with me, I'll do whatever it takes to be with you always."

"So will I." She ran her finger down the seam of her uniform opening, relishing the way his dark gaze locked on each bit of skin slowly revealed. Relishing the wonder and need he didn't even try to hide. "There may be some challenges ahead, but I believe in us. There's nothing coming so bad that we haven't already faced on Dragath25. Together."

He laced his palms with hers, drawing her close, skin to skin. "Wherever we are, Bella, wherever we go, you'll always be my home."

She hadn't expected to find something so beautiful or perfect on Dragath25, but there it was. A thousand questions remained about Earth's future, about Ava's fate, about Caine's sentence, but she knew they'd deal with them as best they could. She and Caine had been tested by Dragath25, and they'd emerged stronger and better. United by a bond that could never be broken.

From the seeds of destruction and danger, something miraculous had grown.

EPILOGUE

"Bella." The furious roar shook the barrack walls.

Bella crouched low. *Left up. Weight even.*

A blur of movement streaked by her hiding space.

She leapt, her palms connecting with solid, warm flesh. By rote, her arm hooked round his throat—for an instant. Then there was only air.

Damn. He'd feinted left.

With a curse, she went sailing overhead, the hard floor coming up fast.

She squeezed her eyes shut, bracing for impact. Only to be spared. Powerful arms hauled her close, twisting them both in midair. She landed with a grunt atop a hard body. Per usual, Caine had taken the brunt of the fall.

"I almost had you that time." Breathing fast, she stared down at the bottomless black eyes she couldn't do without. Her heart gave that same flutter it always did when she saw him, her skin beginning that slow burn. Nearly eight months later, Caine still drove her wild with just a look. He may have been dressed in the trappings of Council civility, but he'd never quite shed that dangerous wildness he'd had since the day they met.

"Almost." Caine lifted his gorgeous head and kissed the tip of her nose. "You're getting better."

"I've had a good teacher." Plus, she'd been practicing like a maniac. For precisely this moment. Her gaze dropped to the disc in his hand, the distinctive gold seal of the Council hard to miss. "That for us?"

The disc bent in his grip. "I told you not yet."

She shrugged. She wasn't afraid of Caine or his bark. She knew the reason behind his gruffness now. His history. His instincts. His ingrained need to protect her. They were just some of the many things she loved and appreciated about him. But she also knew he wouldn't let his fears rule either of them. They'd come to trust each other too much to let the past stand in their way.

"Ava has already waited too long for us to come and find her." Bella's heart still hurt every time she thought of her missing friend, of how she must think she'd been abandoned, when the reality was totally different. "I know you're as sickened as me by all the Command Council delays and excuses. It's way past time to take this on ourselves."

Bella didn't know what kind of shape her friend would be in when they found her, but she knew Ava would never have stopped fighting for her freedom. After dealing with her friend's family and fiancé, Bella had a better idea of the source of her friend's strength—and her wounds.

Besides a meek mother with sad eyes and a bruise on her chin, Bella had found the rest of Ava's relations arrogant, despicable, and creepy to the core. They'd flat out told her and Caine to mind their own business when they offered to help. It was clear from the way they spoke—as if Ava was a possession to be retrieved—that they were committed to recovering her, but that the homecoming wouldn't be a happy one.

Before meeting them, Bella had thought Council families were the lucky ones.

"Ava deserves the freedom she always wanted. She's not going to get that if her family finds her first."

"You're right." Caine's head clunked back against the floor. "It is past time. For her. And for us. Besides, even tigos and pythiles aren't as dangerous as those asshole Council members."

Actual jokes. Caine had been making them more and more.

Her heartbeat picked up a notch. "So we're a go?"

His sigh was long and loud. "You'll probably be a hell of a lot safer once we're off this planet anyway."

He wasn't wrong. She wasn't exactly the Command Council's favorite person thanks to her recent maneuvering—and not just over Ava.

Living up to her fighter girl nickname, she'd used the insider information Winthrop had given her about the Command Council's growing precarious leadership position along with her findings about Dragath25 soil to blackmail the Council into pardoning Caine. It hadn't been easy. Council members preferred to protect their own. But when faced with the possibility of losing out on information about potential food and water sources that could help them retain power, they'd tossed aside one of their own easily enough.

Of course, she hadn't stopped there. She'd also used the information to wrestle better food and lodging for all non-Council people. Nothing revolutionary, but enough to make things a little more fair. And put a dent in established protocol. Something few in the Council welcomed.

Which was why Caine was so worried about Council reprisal. He'd been doling out his share of intimidating looks during the mandatory Council meetings. And though he hadn't mentioned it to her, she knew he'd engaged in more than a few physical 'discussions' in the corridors with displeased Councilmen and their hired muscle. All to keep her safe.

"And you once thought Dragath25 was the most dangerous place in the solar system," she teased.

He snorted.

She kissed the corner of his lip, pleased to see the hint of a laugh line at the edge of his mouth. It was a good sign.

Despite the issues with the Council, he was happy. They were happy.

Though he'd grumbled and protested about risking herself for his sake, she could tell a weight had been lifted since his pardon had come through. Reuniting with extended family and friends had also gone a long way to healing old wounds. But what had really made him smile was when Councilman Hendricks and his brother were found guilty of over fifteen counts of murder. They were already serving triple life sentences on, irony of ironies, a new penal colony rumored to be even harsher than Dragath25. Gwen had finally been given justice.

Now another woman needed them to fight for her.

"A sanctioned shuttle is being prepared for our use. Supplies and food included." Bella kissed the other side of his mouth. "Council clearly wants me off this planet as soon as possible."

This time he didn't laugh. A new sadness had entered his gaze. "Hunter and Chloe aren't going to be happy. They've gotten used to having you around." And Caine had gotten used to being around her brother and sister as well. After so much time alone, he was clearly enjoying being part of a larger family.

"Did you read the full assignment?" she asked.

A sheepish look surfaced on Caine's face. "Only the first paragraph saying we'd been cleared to return to Dragath25 air space to look for Cadet Davies. After that…I, ah, stopped reading and took off to find you."

So he could roar at her for speeding things along.

"Well then," she said, happy she could give him the good news, "you're going to be pleased. Hunter and Chloe have been cleared to come as well." At eighteen, Hunter was almost as tall as Caine and, thanks to better access to food, finally starting to lose the gaunt look that had always worried her. Chloe, too, looked healthier than ever, her blossoming beauty garnering more than her share of looks. As big sister, she would have worried about leaving them behind again, but thanks to their training in piloting and astrophysics respectively, she didn't have to.

Satisfaction swelled within. Her family. Whole. Healthy. Together. After so much struggle. She couldn't be more grateful.

Of course, she wasn't a fool. She'd lived on Dragath25 before. She understood there were risks to returning. But she had no choice. Her friend needed her. And what's more, scratching out an existence on Earth under strict Council rule didn't hold the same appeal it once had. Not when she'd learned there was so much more life could offer.

This time, though, they'd be returning to a planet plunged in battle. After hearing her report on the Oasis and Caine's testimony regarding 225 and his pack, the Council had declared war. Hundreds of soldiers had descended on Dragath25, too many for 225's jammers to affect. Thousands of prisoners had been slaughtered, but there were still substantial pockets of resistance, and 225 had yet to be caught or killed. Dragath25 remained a dangerous, lawless place.

As if he read her mind, Caine ran a finger across her brow, smoothing out her worry lines. "Don't worry, I'm not going to let anything happen to you or your siblings—and we're going to find your friend. Whatever it takes."

Steady once again, she wrapped her arms around his wide chest. "I'm not going to let anything happen to you, either." She kissed his lips hard and fast. "We're going to be better than fine."

"Together," he agreed.

Love and hope surged through her. Sure, the future was unknown and there were challenges yet to face, but with Caine by her side, she knew she could handle anything. Together, they could find pleasure and joy and beauty anywhere. That's what love made possible, even on Dragath25.

Thank you for reading *Trapped: Book One in the Condemned series*! I hope you enjoyed it. If you did, please help other readers find this book:

1. Help other people find this book by writing a review.

2. **Sign up** for new release emails and my newsletter by contacting me at www.alisonaimes.com

3. Come like my Facebook page at http://www.facebook.com/alisonaimesauthor

Want to know what happened to Cadet Ava Davies after her disappearance from Dragath25? Read an excerpt from:

TAKEN,
Book Two in the Condemned Series
by Alison Aimes.

CHAPTER ONE

She was caught. Her arms pinned to the wall. Her legs, too. Every limb twisted at an impossible angle. No manacles necessary. Just the cruel indifference of spinning, plummeting centrifugal force.

Cadet Ava Davies struggled to get air past the acrid terror squeezing her lungs. One minute she'd been hustling down one of a million rocky cliffs on Dragath25 toward fellow junior scientist and friend Bella West, her mind racing with the implications of her recent soil findings, the guard Pratt grim-faced and unfriendly at her side, and then…nothing.

She'd woken up here. To searing heat. Her head spinning. Her jaw throbbing while her stomach plunged, her right cheek slammed into the wall, and her mouth contorted into a shocked O. Around her, ear-shattering screams ricocheted through the small space while dim bile-colored lights flickered overhead and twisted bodies flashed in and out of visibility.

Where in God's name was she?

"Davies?....What…happening?" The sound of her name startled her. The voice came from behind.

A shameful wave of relief crashed through her.

Though the sound was distorted, she recognized the speaker. Pratt. The soldier assigned to guard her while she collected soil samples. Like the rest of the Command Council soldiers assigned to protect the scientists, he'd never warmed to her. Nor she to him. Still, right now, his familiar voice was the most beautiful thing she'd ever heard.

"Pratt..." It was hard getting the words out, the force of the drop driving her tongue to the roof of her mouth. "No...idea."

"Hear...me?" Pratt's distorted voice had grown shriller. "Help!"

"No...panic." Even knowing it was futile, she tried to turn. She only succeeded in exhausting herself further. "Nothing...to do." She let her muscles go slack. It offered no change in her position, but it did conserve energy. "Other...crew?"

There was a momentary pause. As if Pratt was assessing whatever he could see.

"No." Pratt's single word was laced with despair.

"For...the...better," she pushed out. Whatever this was, it wasn't good. She didn't want Bella or any of the others anywhere near it.

It was almost impossible to believe only two weeks had passed since she'd quietly slipped onto the Academy shuttle, part of the scientific team charged by the Command Council with exploring distant planets for viable plants that could be cultivated on Earth.

Of course, she'd had her own reasons for coming, but she'd been excited to think she might, thanks to her expertise in soil ecosystems, be a part of the team that found a way to save Earth's remaining survivors and break the cycle of famine, blight, and death that had been plaguing their planet since the disappearance of the great forests and the onset of the dust storms.

It would have been a tremendous triumph. Especially for a girl who'd only been allowed to return to school and study such an undignified subject as a twisted punishment. After all, as her esteemed father had said, who better to study dirt than dirt itself?

And if that 'dirt' somehow found her sister Khyla alive…well, that would have been the answer to every prayer she'd had for the last two years.

"Where…are…we?" Pratt's terrified bellow reverberated off the walls.

They were spinning and dropping so fast the walls had begun to shudder. The others' screams grew louder.

"Don't…know." She tried to shout above the noise. Were they still on Dragath25? The heat was all too familiar, but the walls of this container were curved like the transport holds at the non-Council barracks back on Earth. She strained to turn her head a quarter inch. They seemed made of the same dull, gray-flecked metal, too.

Her heart beat a little faster.

Maybe she was crazy, but she almost would have preferred some kind of unfamiliar technology. Anything that might suggest whoever had stuck her on this plummeting hell wasn't human. Because while being the first to encounter alien life might have been dangerous, she already knew how monstrous humans could be.

She shifted her focus to the men in her sight. The flashing light offered up brief glimpses of bodies barely covered in tattered scraps of fabric or nothing at all, their contorted limbs and torsos covered in crude tattoos that looked as rough as the men themselves. Some looked emaciated, the lines of each rib laid bare by the flickering lights. Others had the kind of thick bulk that came from eating more than their share. But one thing was constant. All had *225 PROPERTY* carved somewhere on their skin. The big, bold letters blinking in and out of visibility like some terrible broken sign.

Her heart, already overworked, slammed harder against her ribs.

She knew 225. Bella had mentioned him often enough. He was the leader of the largest Dragath25 prison gang. Which meant the men in her line of sight had likely been his gang-mates, the most notorious of rapists and killers exiled from Earth by the Command Council.

She'd find no allies among them. Only another threat.

"P—pretty." The ominous word issued from the giant whose outstretched hand was an arm's length from her nose

He was staring at her. Or more aptly at the telling Command Council tattoo seared into her neck.

"Going...fuck...then...break...Council...bitch." Though garbled, the giant's underlying threat reached her loud and clear. "Can't....wait...hear...scream." The man's long, matted rust colored hair stood up at all ends, exposing a low sloping forehead, pug-nose, and a raised, white scar that snaked from his eyebrow to the corner of his mouth. His eyes were beady yellow slits glittering with lust and the promise of pain.

It was a look she knew all too well.

She shrank within herself, her mouth going dry, memories turning her blood to ice, shattering in seconds all the progress she'd made these last few months.

Her gaze sank to the floor, obedient, submissive. If not for the force cleaving her to the wall, her body would have followed. Her head bowing, her knees folding under her, her legs sliding wide as was only proper. Compliance the only way to lessen the blows.

You will do as you're told. Strike. The birch cane—an expensive rarity in an era when the forests had long ago disappeared—lashed her back, sending fire licking across her skin, the flimsy silk of her expensive Council robe affording little protection. She didn't need to look up to know her father stood just behind Ren, his expression harsh and unreadable as always. *You will behave in a manner befitting a man in my position.* Strike. Strike. *Do you understand me, Ayanna?* The punishment stick, well-polished and strong despite its advanced age, showed no sign of breaking. No matter how she prayed. But then again, Lead Councilman Ren Hollisworth took exceptional care of every possession he acquired, except perhaps his future wife.

The lurch of the container smacked her back to the present.

She shook off the memory. Buried it deep. The past couldn't touch her now. And whatever happened next, she wasn't Ayanna Talis anymore. She was Cadet Ava Davies, a trained Academy scientist, not some bruised and broken pathetic girl who had no choice but to take it.

"Pratt?" She forced herself to return eye contact with Yellow Eyes. To pretend they both hadn't registered her momentary cowering. "….weapon?"

Pratt's lack of an answer was answer enough.

The killer's outstretched hand twitched, his dirty fingernails stretching toward her.

But she wasn't down for the count yet. If she hadn't been searched before she was stuck in this hold, the small, homemade spear Bella had insisted she carry everywhere was still tucked inside her boot. It might not be enough, but it was something. Yellow Eyes wasn't going to find her the easy target her fiancé had. Her days of folding without a fight were over.

A disembodied, nasal voice filled the hold. "Condemned of Dragath25, you are now the property of the Tribunal."

The hair at the back of her neck prickled. She'd heard that name before.

Around her the others had gone silent.

"Your sole purpose," the voice continued, "is to mine the veins of silver ore found in the caverns. Meet your quota of fifty kitloms per day and you will live. Fail and you will die."

Roars of protest shook the hold.

"Descent will end in forty seconds."

Her breath left in a rush.

Her gaze locked with Yellow Eyes. From the way he looked at her, she didn't think she'd have a chance to make her quota. Frankly, she didn't think she'd survive five minutes past release from the wall.

Time slowed. Blood pulsed through her veins. Her gaze narrowed until all she saw was the twisted half-smile of the threat in front of her.

She'd been here before. She'd done what she must to survive. She would again.

The hold shuddered once more. The lights flickered and went out. And, just like that, the hold lurched to a stop.

She tumbled to the floor, pain winding up her wrists as her hands shot forward, just managing to save her face from slamming into metal. Around her, the thump of other bodies echoed.

She was already fumbling for her spear, her fingers just closing around the precious shaft, when a meaty hand closed round her ankle.

Copyright © 2015 by Orchid, Inc.
Sign up for newsletter at www.alisonaimes.com to be notified when **TAKEN** is ready for release.

ABOUT THE AUTHOR

Alison Aimes is the award-winning author of the sexy sci-fi romance series the Condemned as well as the sizzling contemporary romance Billionaires' Revenge series. A sci-fi fanatic with a PhD in Modern History, she's an all-over-the-map kind of woman whose always had a love for dramatic stories and great books, no matter the era. Now, she's creating her own stories full of intrigue and passion, but always with a happy-ever-after ending. She lives in Maryland with her husband, two kids, and her dog. When not in front of the computer, she can be found hanging with family and friends, hiking, trying to turn herself into a pretzel through yoga, listening to a fabulous TED talk, or, last but not least, sitting on the couch imagining her characters' next great adventures.

Alison can be found online at www.alisonaimes.com

Connect with Alison Aimes:

Website: http://www.alisonaimes.com
Facebook: https://www.facebook/alisonaimes
Twitter: https://twitter.com/alisonaimes

OTHER BOOKS BY ALISON AIMES

IN THE CONDEMNED SERIES:

TRAPPED, March 2016

TAKEN, coming August 2016

Made in the USA
Middletown, DE
11 February 2016